Confidentially
YOURS
The Secret Talent

4

JO WHITTEMORE

Confidentially

YOURS

The Secret Talent

4

HARPER
An Imprint of HarperCollinsPublishers

Library of Congress Control Number: 2016938981
ISBN 978-0-06-235899-8

Typography by Kate J. Engbring
16 17 18 19 20   OPM   10 9 8 7 6 5 4 3 2 1
❖
First Edition

33614057774290

For my sweet Ari,
a man of many talents

Contents

CHAPTER

1

Greek Out

I should've been named Apollo.

I know it's pretty bold comparing myself to the Greek god of light, but Mr. Sunshine and I have a lot in common: We're both Greek, we both have twin sisters, we're both into culture, and we both value honesty more than . . .

Okay, that last one's a stretch. For me, the truth's a gray area, and whether I tell it depends on how much I'll suffer.

For example, if a girl asks, "Does this shirt look stupid?," I'm never going to tell the truth. Ever.

Because I did once.

Getting hit with a bag hurts a lot more than you'd think.

Anyway, apart from the fact that Apollo was a god and I'm mortal, we're practically the same guy.

"Practically," I said to the crumbling marble statue in front of me. Poor Apollo was missing an arm, half his face, and a leg. "Although, you seem a little more accident-prone."

"There is *no* way you saw me smack into that display case," said a voice beside me. "I was all the way across the room!"

I grinned and turned to my friend Vanessa Jackson, who was cradling one hand with the other. Our history class was on a field trip to the Berryville art museum, and we were all given specific instructions not to touch *anything*.

Those words have no meaning to a group of twelve-year-olds.

"I wasn't talking to you," I said. "But let me guess. You tried to reach through the glass?"

Poor V tends to be a little on the clumsy side.

"It's just so clear!" she said, massaging her fingers. Then she looked up at Apollo. "I'm guessing you were talking to this guy. That's cool. Sometimes I talk to my dummy."

I gasped in mock horror. "What a mean thing to call your brother!"

Vanessa giggled and punched my arm with her good hand. "No! My dressmaker's dummy."

V designs and makes her own clothes. I'm no fashion expert, but from what I've seen, she seems to know her stuff. There's never an extra neck hole or anything.

Her style savvy is probably why her answers for the advice column are so popular. Vanessa and I, along with our friends Heather Schwartz and Brooke Jacobs, answer cries for help in "Lincoln's Letters," the advice column for Abraham

Lincoln Middle School's newspaper, the *Lincoln Log*.

V dishes fashion advice, Heather gives friendship and relationship advice, and Brooke tackles health and fitness. I, Tim Antonides, round it out by providing the male perspective on issues, but to be honest, sometimes I wish I did health and fitness instead. Sports are a huge part of my life, and there's never a season when I'm not in some sort of uniform. Brooke is a sports nut too, but she can't give the guy's point of view like I can.

For now, I settle with being the secondary sportswriter. The stories I'm assigned aren't that interesting ("Football Team Gets New Footballs!"), but I'm working really hard to impress so that someday I can be bumped up to head sportswriter.

"You talk to your dressmaker's dummy?" I asked V. "It doesn't even have a head."

"Oh, because if it did, there'd be a better

chance of me getting an answer?" she asked, laughing again.

For Vanessa, everything is a reason to laugh. She's one of the most upbeat people I know.

"Yeah, okay," I said. Then I pointed to Apollo. "Did you know that Apollo could see the future?"

"Neat. Did he see you getting left behind because everyone else is in the next room?" Vanessa asked, pointing toward an archway.

I glanced around. Other than Vanessa, not a single other person from class was with us.

"Oops," I said. "Let's go."

We jogged out of the room to catch up with our classmates, who were checking out an exhibit on Polynesia.

". . . live in Hawaii today," our history teacher, Mr. Edwards, finished. He nodded to me. "Good of you to finally leave Greece and join us, Mr. Antonides."

I gave him an apologetic shrug. "My chariot had a flat."

I'm usually running late to stuff, so it's handy to keep a pocketful of excuses.

Mr. E smiled and gestured to another exhibit. "Dance is a large part of Polynesian culture. It is a way for them to tell stories, give thanks to the gods, and celebrate life in general."

"Ha! Check it out." A guy in our class pointed to a screen showing a video of a Polynesian dance.

I wouldn't say the advice column has any real enemies, but if we did, this kid Ryan Durstwich would be the closest thing. When our very first issue came out, he argued that Brooke, a girl, shouldn't give sports advice. Then he went on to try to take her job at the newspaper, saying he could do better, which ended in an advice-off. *And* every time he catches me reading a book, he makes fun of the title, like referring to *The Wind in the Willows* as *The Wind from My Butt.*

So yeah, I'm not a Ryan fan.

The entire class gathered to watch the video of the Polynesian men who were hooting and hopping around.

"All the guys are wearing skirts," Ryan said with a laugh. "They look dorky."

"Hey!" cried Vanessa at the same time I said, "That's not dorky!"

Everyone's attention shifted from the video to V and me.

"I just started dating a guy from Hawaii . . . Gil Pendleton," explained Vanessa. "And if he wore a grass skirt, I wouldn't care." She frowned. "Unless he matched it with the wrong shirt."

Several people laughed.

"What about you?" A guy next to me, Berkeley Dennis, bumped my arm. "You seem almost as mad as Vanessa."

"Me?" I repeated.

Okay, so here's the thing.

I'm a Greek folk dancer. Sometimes our costumes have skirts. And tights. And shoes with fluffy pompoms on the toes. It doesn't look very cool, especially for the dance numbers when the guys hold hands and skip in a circle. Only five people at school know my secret, one of them being my sister, Gabby, but only because she dances too.

But nobody else is ever going to find out.

Especially not Berkeley Dennis.

Think of the coolest, sportiest, dudeliest guy you know. Now have him sitting on a pile of money. That's Berkeley.

I mentioned earlier that our advice column was pretty popular, and it gets me a lot of attention from the girls. Needless to say, a lot of guys don't like that. Ordinarily, I wouldn't care, but my best friend, Gus McDade, moved away over the summer, so I've been searching for new people to hang out with. Berkeley and I have a few classes together, and he helped rescue my shorts from the swimming pool when someone threw them in (seriously, the guys are *jealous*), so he's at the top of my potential friend list. But I had a feeling he wouldn't be if he knew of my frolicking ways.

As soon as Berkeley asked about my outburst, Ryan chimed in.

"Yeah, why does it bother you so much?" he asked with a smirk. "Do you dance around in a skirt too?"

The other kids snickered.

Nope. Nobody else was *ever* going to find out.

"Actually, I agree with Vanessa," I said in my calmest, coolest voice. "It's important to respect people's backgrounds. Just like I'd never insult *your* family for swinging from trees and scratching their armpits."

Everyone in the class roared with laughter. Except Ryan.

"Oh yeah?" he said. "Well, *your* family . . . They're . . ."

"Capable of complete sentences?" I finished for him. "Don't worry, Ape Man, you'll get there someday."

More laughter until Mr. E quieted everyone down. "Why don't we move on to Polynesian art?"

We all followed him into the next room, and Berkeley bumped my arm again. "Way to put him in his place."

"He's had it coming," I said. "Believe me."

He nodded. "Listen, my cousin Alistair's coming to town the weekend before Christmas, and a bunch of guys will be at my house to meet him. You should come."

I froze in my tracks, causing Vanessa to walk into me from behind.

"Sorry!" she said.

I didn't respond to her. I was too busy staring openmouthed at Berkeley.

"Alistair, as in Alistair Dennis? Your cousin is Alistair 'Adrenaline' Dennis?" I finally managed.

Berkeley grinned. "Well, to me, he's just Alistair, but yeah."

"Who's that?" asked V.

"Who's . . ." I regarded her with an expression of disbelief. "He's only one of the best motocross riders ever! He can do a front fender grab with Indian air and end with a no footer on a single jump."

"Wow, cool!" Vanessa bounced up and down. "What's motocross?"

I held up a hand to block her out and turned to Berkeley. "I would *love* to go, dude."

He nodded. "I'll have you added to the guest list."

He hurried to catch up with his friends, and I

turned to Vanessa with a huge smile.

"I get to meet Adrenaline Dennis!" I pumped the air with my fist.

She clapped. "I still have no idea what moto-cross is!"

"Oh, sorry," I said. "Motorcycle racing. All those other things I mentioned were different tricks."

"Neat!" She gave me a thumbs-up. "And thanks for helping me stick up for Gil earlier."

I checked the area and stepped closer. "I wasn't sticking up for him, actually. I was doing it for myself."

"Oh, right. Because of your . . ." She lifted an imaginary skirt hem and started high kicking.

I sighed. "We don't dance like that, but yes."

She shook her head. "I don't know why you're keeping this a big secret. I mean, you're dancing in some Christmas show. Everyone's going to find out."

"I'm not dancing in just any Christmas show," I corrected her. "I'm performing for Christmas Around the World at the Museum of Science and Industry in Chicago! And I promise you, nobody from our school is going to go. It would mean expressing an interest in culture."

Vanessa stuck her tongue out. "You know what? The Three Musketeers were *going* to go, but now we won't."

The Three Musketeers were what she, Brooke, and Heather called themselves. They've been best friends since kindergarten. Now that Gus was gone, I envied that. The longest other friendship I've had is with Gabby, but she's not exactly one of the guys. Even if I draw a mustache on her, she's still a girl . . . just an angrier one.

"Well, thank you for the support," I told V, "but I'd rather not have the three of you giggling in the front row."

"We wouldn't!" she said, looking insulted. Then she stared into space and giggled.

I sighed again. "You're thinking about me dancing, aren't you?"

She stifled her laughter behind a hand. "No. I was thinking about . . . um . . . motocross."

A girl from our class walked toward us. "Hey, Mr. E says the Polynesians settled Hawaii faster than you two can cross a room."

"Sorry," I said. "We were busy picking coconuts."

"You're so funny!" The girl giggled and then ran back to the rest of the class.

Vanessa rolled her eyes and pushed me forward. "If we had coconuts, I would've knocked you over the head with one long ago."

I flashed a smile. "What can I say? I've got a way with the ladies."

Except when it comes to my editor in chief, Mary Patrick Stephens.

Once upon a time I would've described Mary Patrick as a wolverine in a skirt, but she's one of the few people who knows and understands my secret dancing life. I've since downgraded her to a honey badger. Because that's what she constantly does: badger us.

As soon as our history class walked back into the school building, Mary Patrick was waiting by the front doors, tapping her foot at a rapid pace.

"You're going to wear a hole in the carpet, you know." I pointed to the floor.

She glanced down. "Who says I haven't already?"

"What's up?" asked Vanessa.

"Brooke is being impossible!" She stamped her foot.

"Actually, she can't be impossible, because by the very nature of her *being* . . ." I stopped after seeing the toxic look from Mary Patrick.

Vanessa put a hand on Mary Patrick's arm. "Explain," she said.

"I asked her to come up with a special advice idea for our holiday issue since winter break is only a couple weeks away. She suggested a column on how to relax because she said I could use it!" Mary Patrick threw her hands into the air.

This time I was smart enough *not* to respond.

"We'll talk to her," Vanessa promised, pulling me toward the hall.

"Actually, I can't," I said. "My uncle's picking me and Gabby up."

"Oh, right!" Mary Patrick said so loudly both Vanessa and I jumped. "Because you're building a house for orphans!" She gave an exaggerated wink.

I winced and stepped closer. "I appreciate the effort at secrecy, but maybe keep the cover-up simple?"

"Gotcha," said Mary Patrick with another

wink. Then in a louder voice, "HAVE FUN AT THE ZOO!"

I gave Vanessa a pained look, and she stifled a giggle. "I'll talk to *her* too," she whispered.

With Christmas only weeks away, it was crunch time for dance rehearsals, so Uncle Theo showed up after school a few times a week to take me and Gabby to the studio. Luckily, it was in a building on the edge of town, so no one from school was going to see me, but I still hurried inside every time my uncle parked the car.

"He's so motivated to dance!" Uncle Theo crowed after me that Thursday. "Get your Greek on, my boy!"

I cringed and pulled my gym bag up closer to my face.

Out of my entire family, Uncle Theo is the proudest of our heritage. The man will use any excuse to bring up Greece. One time, I was lacing my baseball cleats, which happened to be

Nikes, and Uncle Theo said, "You know, Nike was the goddess of victory. She's probably the reason you play so well, watching over every pitch you throw."

For the entire game, I swear I felt someone right behind me.

As soon as I stepped into the dance building, I lowered my bag and froze.

Girls. Cute ones. They wore tap shoes and leotards and were talking to a woman with a scarf tied around her neck. One of the girls looked over at me and smiled. I smiled back.

At that moment, the door behind me opened and Uncle Theo's voice boomed out. "Timotheos!" he cried, using the Greek version of my name. "You should be dancing your way down the hall."

Instantly, my entire body tensed.

"Please, no," I muttered.

I spun around to see Uncle Theo bouncing

toward me, giant mustache twitching. I caught
Gabby's eye and silently pleaded with her to stop
him before he could say something embarrassing
like—

"By the way, you dropped your tights in the
parking lot."

He held up a pair of white stockings. It took
me less than five seconds to snatch them out of
his hand and cram them into the pocket of my
jeans.

"You dance in tights?" one of the girls asked,
her smile getting even bigger.

"Oh, not just tights!" said Uncle Theo.

"So where do you go to school?" I asked her,
by way of obvious topic change. "I'm at Abraham
Lincoln."

Uncle Theo was now standing beside me so
that I was caught in the gravitational pull of his
humiliation. "Tim dances in full costume! They
both do!" He gestured to Gabby as well.

I glanced at my sister.

There's a theory that twins can communicate telepathically, and Gabby and I have tested it many times. One time we got pretty close, when I projected an image of money and then took a box of her Girl Scouts cookies, but she said mental dollars weren't a real form of payment.

Regardless, I needed us to be mentally linked now more than ever. Luckily, Gabby nodded at me and rubbed her arms.

"Is it chilly in here?" She looked at me. "Should we go warm up in the studio?"

I tugged on Uncle Theo's sleeve. "Yeah, we probably should." I waved to the girls. "Later!"

But Uncle Theo was determined to Greek out. "You two won't be cold if you dance a little sirtaki," he said with a chuckle. He winked at the girl I was talking to. "You should see this young man move."

And then . . . the ultimate humiliation.

Uncle Theo snapped his fingers. "What am I thinking? I actually have a video of it on my phone!" He reached into his back pocket. By this point, the other girl had rejoined her friend.

Misery loves company.

"Oh, they don't want to see that," I said with a nervous laugh, stepping between my uncle and the girls.

"Of course they do! Don't you, girls?" Uncle Theo held out his phone so they had no choice but to look, and he started the video.

The camerawork was a little shaky, but there I was, holding the wrists of a guy to my right and a guy to my left as we shuffled sideways in a circle, occasionally kicking our legs out.

Sadly, I realized Vanessa's imitation hadn't been too far off.

"I don't understand," one of the girls said with a furrowed brow. "Are you standing behind one of these dancing women?"

"Um . . . I'm that . . . that dancing woman," I said, pointing at the screen.

She let out a laugh. "Oh my God."

"Isn't that something?" Uncle Theo asked, mistaking her amusement for awe.

"Oh, it's something all right," she said, linking arms with her friend. "Excuse us. My mom's waiting outside."

I cringed and avoided her eyes, but I couldn't ignore the giggles and whispers that followed them out of the building. I didn't look up until I heard the door close, and when I did, it was to see Uncle Theo rewatching the video with a proud smile.

"You've got style, my boy!"

"Uh . . . thanks." I cleared my throat. "Hey, Uncle Theo?"

He glanced up, the video on his phone still playing so I could hear rhythmic clapping and the strumming of a lyre.

"What is it, Timotheos?" he asked.

"You know how you tell strangers—the mail carrier, the dentist, anyone eating an olive—about me being a Greek folk dancer? Maybe you could do a little less of that." I pinched my fingers together. "And by a little less, I mean never again."

Uncle Theo lowered his phone. "What?"

"Oooh." Beside me, Gabby sucked in her breath. "I'm gonna go change," she whispered, shuffling out of Uncle Theo's line of sight.

Uncle Theo stared at me.

"What I mean," I said, squirming under his gaze, "is that not everybody needs to hear about what a great dancer I am."

His expression relaxed. "Ah. I'm bragging too much. It embarrasses you."

"Uh . . . yeah, something like that," I said.

He tapped the side of his nose and winked at me. "Say no more. Although, you shouldn't be so modest about your talent, Tim! Few men can twirl a baton the way you can!"

I winced and glanced around, but we were alone. "Thanks, but can we just keep that fact in the family for now?"

"Of course," Uncle Theo said with a nod. He checked the time on his phone. "We should get changed."

Gabby walked out of the women's restroom while we were walking into the men's. I stopped and let Uncle Theo go in without me.

"Hey, thanks for the support earlier," I told my sister, laying on the sarcasm. "It really meant a lot." I patted my chest.

Gabby made a face. "Sorry. You know how I feel about confrontation."

"You confront me all the time," I argued.

"That's different. You're my brother. Fighting with you is second nature. Whenever I see your face, I just want to . . ." She held up a clenched fist.

"Punch the air with joy?" I finished.

She grinned. "Look, it's really not a big deal that you're a Greek folk dancer," she said. "Those girls were dumb."

"Easy for you to say! You're a girl. Nobody freaks if you wear a skirt and prance about."

She smirked. "When have you ever seen me prance?"

"Whatever," I said. "You say it's not a big deal, but the reaction from those girls says otherwise. Greek folk dancing isn't going to be making its way into any music videos."

Gabby snorted and waved a dismissive hand. "Who cares? You really want to date someone who's going to think less of you for pursuing a passion?"

"Greek folk dancing isn't my passion!"

Through the restroom door I could hear Uncle Theo coughing, so I lowered my voice. "Look, I don't know how much longer I can keep doing this. Dancing was fun in kindergarten, and it was tolerable in elementary because people threw money, but now that we're in middle school, I've got a reputation to think about!"

Gabby rolled her eyes. "Right, right. I forgot that you're the poster boy for cool. Tell me again . . . Did you find your gym shorts in the shallow or deep end of the pool?"

I pointed at her. "And if the guys at school knew I dressed in silly costumes and sometimes danced with my sister, it wouldn't just be my shorts in the pool. It'd be me."

"Then thank goodness you can swim," she said.

Uncle Theo emerged from the restroom and I went in, changing as fast as possible. When I was in full dress, I poked my head out to make sure nobody was around and then sprinted to the studio where Gabby, Uncle Theo, and several other Greek dancers were already waiting.

The choreographer greeted us, started the music, and we fell into formation. I had to admit, the upbeat tempo was pretty hard to keep out of my body, and soon, I was bouncing along and clapping with everyone else. When rehearsal was over, it didn't even bother me that Uncle Theo wrapped me in a sweaty bear hug.

"I could see you feeling the music! That's my Timotheos!" he said. He was so happy, in fact, that he took me and Gabby to get frozen yogurt at the shop next door.

There are a few different yogurt shops around town, but my favorite has a bookstore next to it. I can grab a book and then a yogurt at Eat Your Words, where all the flavors are named after book titles. My favorite flavor is Chocolate War, which is milk chocolate with a dark-chocolate swirl in the center.

I started in on my cup while Gabby got her Grapes of Wrath and Uncle Theo got Crime and Punishmint.

From where I sat, I could see the list of flavors on the wall, which I'd read at least a hundred times. Behind me, I heard the kaching of the cash register and Uncle Theo asking the cashier, "Is that a Nike T-shirt you're wearing?"

I shook my head and smiled to myself while I checked my phone. I had a couple new group texts from Brooke, Heather, and Vanessa about ideas for our pre-Christmas issue . . . and one from Berkeley Dennis!

Saturday before Christmas, 5:00 p.m.

1031 Vanderbilt Place

Can you make it?

A chance to meet Adrenaline Dennis and possibly make friends who wouldn't send my clothes for a swim? Of course I could make it! I'd wrestle alligators and cross a river of lava to make it.

I was just about to respond when a new text popped up from an unknown number.

It contained only three words and one image.

Hey, Twinkle Toes.

The image was of me at dance practice.

CHAPTER 2

Twinkle-Toes Tim

I flipped my phone facedown, but the text still flashed bright as a supernova in my mind.

Hey, Twinkle Toes.

I'd never told anyone this, but I had big dreams of becoming president someday. The name Twinkle-Toes Tim could *not* follow me into the Oval Office.

With a nervous glance around, I turned the phone back over and studied the picture that followed the text message. From the wild state of my hair, I'd say it was taken in the last hour (I use nine-to-five hair gel, and it pretty much gives up right on schedule). Plus, the particular move I was doing was part of the *kalamatiano*, the final dance we'd practiced. Why, oh, why had I insisted on throwing in a twirl?

Someone had followed me all the way across town. Or they'd been lucky enough to catch me in the wrong place at the wrong time. Had I done anything else embarrassing, like pick my nose? Were they still watching me now?

I scanned the room. Other than my family, the only person in the yogurt shop was a man who looked so old he was probably still sending messages by telegraph.

I picked up my phone, fingers flying across the screen as I texted the mystery number.

Who is this?

A couple minutes went by. The old man snored at his table. Chocolate War melted in my cup. Then the response:

You'll find out tomorrow.

"Nope," I muttered. "I'll find out now." I dialed the number, but the mystery texter refused to pick up. Smart.

Not so smart? Forgetting to change his voice-mail greeting.

"What uuup? It's Ryan. I'm way too busy to answer, so leave me a message." His voice took on a forced casualness. "Or don't. Whatever."

Ryan Durstwich. I should've figured.

The voice mail beeped, and I started talking. "Wow, Ryan, cool greeting. This is Tim, by the way. You know . . . the guy you've been sending creepy messages to?" Gabby was walking toward me so I spoke in a softer voice. "I'm not scared of you, and if you want to go up against me, you'd better bring your A game."

I ended the call and stared at the picture of myself again.

At least my arms looked good.

Gabby dropped into a seat across from me, eyes shining. "Mom and Dad are making lobster mac 'n' cheese tonight!"

One of the best parts of having parents who own grocery stores is no shortage of good food. Normally, I'd be just as excited as she was, but at the moment I was distracted by Ryan's texts.

"Awesome," I said, giving my sister a thumbs-up.

My phone chimed with a new message from Ryan.

You aren't scared yet, but you will be.

"Who's that?" asked Gabby, tilting her head to read my screen.

"Nobody," I said, pocketing the phone. "Some girl I met today."

Gabby rolled her eyes. "Another one? Would you get a girlfriend already?"

I shook my head. "It's too close to Christmas.

If it didn't work out, her present would be a breakup." I stood and tossed my yogurt cup into the trash. "Ready to go?"

Gabby looked toward the garbage. "You only took, like, one bite, *and* you're not excited about lobster mac 'n' cheese? What's going on with you?"

"Nothing," I said. "My stomach just hurts from all the dancing."

"Oh." She made a face. "Well, sit in the front seat on the way home. I don't want you barfing on me."

"How did I ever get so lucky in the sister department?" I asked.

She smiled and went to grab Uncle Theo. On the way out to the car, he put his arm around my shoulders and squeezed.

"Are you okay, Timotheos? You hardly touched your yogurt."

I shrugged and smiled. "What can I say? It's

Greek yogurt or *no* yogurt."

Uncle Theo chuckled and ruffled my hair. "Always the comedian."

He and Gabby talked about ways to improve our biggest dance number for the museum performance while I peered out the window.

What I'd told Ryan was true; I wasn't scared of him. But the more time I had to think, the more I started to wonder what exactly he was planning. He wouldn't post that picture of me all over school. That'd be too easy for me to explain away. I could just tell people I was goofing around. Ryan had to know at least that much.

I hated to admit it, but I'd have to do what he said, and wait.

Uncle Theo pulled his car into the driveway, and Gabby leaped out, racing to the front door.

"Lobster mac! Lobster mac!" she cried.

Her excitement was contagious, and I found myself hurrying up the driveway too.

Gabby left the front door open, and the smell of baked cheese wafted from the kitchen on warm currents of air. The scent enveloped me and slipped past, carrying worries about Ryan with them. Then Uncle Theo's arm wrapped around my middle, and he hoisted me off the ground, lugging me under one arm.

"Hey!" I said with a laugh. "I'm not a football."

"You can say that again. Oof!" He dropped me onto the carpet just outside the kitchen, where my parents were darting back and forth doing last-minute meal prep.

"Incoming bread crumbs!" Mom called to Dad seconds before she threw him the canister. Luckily, Dad turned just in time to catch it between his oven-mitted hands. He nodded to me, Gabby, and Uncle Theo.

"Hey, guys. You're just in time. And I hope you're hungry." He sprinkled the bread crumbs over a gooey, melty bed of yellow and red. Then he popped the lobster mac back into the oven.

"We had frozen yogurt, but I can still eat," Gabby said, hopping up onto a stool.

"Theo!" Mom bumped the fridge shut with her hip, a bowl of salad and a dressing bottle in her hands. "What have I told you about giving the kids sweets before dinner?" She raised an eyebrow at her brother.

Uncle Theo grinned. "That it's an excellent way to make them like me?"

She rolled her eyes. "Are you staying for dinner?"

"I wish I could," he said, "but *I've* got a date tonight." Uncle Theo puffed out his chest and smiled broadly.

"Nice! Try only talking about Greece every *other* sentence," Mom said, smirking at him. "Tim, honey, can you get the salad tongs?"

I grabbed them while Uncle Theo kissed Gabby on the forehead. "Good-bye, *matakia mou*. And you too," he said, ruffling my hair again. "I'll see you both on Saturday." He waved to Mom and Dad and then was gone.

"I hope his date goes well," Gabby said after he left. "And that she doesn't notice his shirt is on backward."

"What?" Mom looked up from the salad she was tossing. "Why on Earth didn't you tell him?"

"Because if he wore it frontward, his date would see the huge yogurt stain," I chimed in.

"Oh good grief." Mom rolled her eyes.

"Well, it can only go uphill from there," Dad said, squeezing Mom's shoulder.

"Unless he shows her one of his dance videos," I said.

"Be nice." Dad set the oven timer. "You share the same heritage and do the same dances."

"Yeah, but *I'm* not over-the-top about it." I took the bowl of salad Mom offered me and popped a tomato into my mouth. Now that I was in the safety and comfort of my own home, my appetite was making a comeback. "Speaking of over-the-top, do you guys know who Alistair Dennis is?"

Mom pursed her lips thoughtfully. "The inventor of the selfie stick?"

At the same time, Dad said, "Adrenaline Dennis? Of course!"

My parents looked at each other.

"Really?" Dad asked Mom. "Selfie stick?"

She shrugged. "Tim said over-the-top! What's crazier than needing to take a picture of yourself that badly?" She batted her eyelashes and held an invisible phone at arm's length.

Dad took her hand and kissed it.

"Gross," said Gabby.

"You think kissing is gross?" asked Dad. "I used to change your diapers."

"Do *not* elaborate on that when we're about to eat," Mom warned him.

"Besides, it's not kissing that's gross," I said, patting Dad's shoulder. "It's you guys."

Dad looked at Mom again. "We make them lobster mac 'n' cheese, and this is the thanks we get."

"Thaaank youuu!" Gabby and I singsonged at the same time.

I carried the salad into the dining room, and Dad followed with a bowl of rolls. "Anyway, what's with Adrenaline Dennis? Did he break some new record?"

I shook my head. "He's going to be in town in a couple weeks, and his cousin Berkeley goes to my school. Berkeley's having a party the weekend before Christmas and asked if I wanted to meet Adrenaline."

Dad raised his eyebrows. "Seriously? That's awesome!" He cleared his throat. "Did your friend happen to mention if any adult chaperones were needed?"

I grinned, both at the chaperone comment and the mention of Berkeley as my friend. I hadn't thought of it that way, but it was kind of cool, imagining myself hanging with other guys.

"Wait a minute," Mom said, peeking in from the kitchen. "What time is this meeting with the Avengers?"

"Adrenaline," Dad and I said together.

"Sorry." Mom held up her hands. "I'm only asking in case it interferes with Christmas Around the World."

"It won't." I crossed my heart. "That's early in the afternoon, and the party is at five. I can go, right?"

She nodded. "Sure."

I grinned and went over to hug her just as the oven timer buzzed.

"Make way!" said Dad. "I'm about to dive face first into this lobster mac."

"I know you're only partly joking," Mom

called after him, "but please remember the cheese will burn your eyelids off!"

After the table was completely set, the four of us settled around it, and there was silence for several minutes as we devoured dinner. Dad was the first to come up for air.

"So, how was the museum?" he asked me. Then he smiled. "Like I have to ask. They should make you honorary curator. Let you run the whole place."

"It was great," I said. "But I don't want to be curator. That's not where the money's at."

"And how would you know?" Mom asked with an amused look.

"I asked the guy how much he makes."

"Oh, Tim," Dad said with a sigh.

"What? He didn't have to answer," I pointed out.

"It's not a polite question," said Mom. "How

would you like it if someone pried into *your* personal life?"

I lowered the forkful of mac 'n' cheese that had been en route to my mouth. For a split second I considered telling them about the text from Ryan, but I was too old to be running to Mommy and Daddy for help.

All I said was, "You're right. How was work?"

My parents told Gabby and me a story about one of their shops that had a goose attacking people at the door. Midway through the tale, I felt my phone buzz in my pocket. I reached for it, and Mom gave me an admonishing look.

"No phones at dinner."

I left it in my pocket, even though all I wanted to do was dive under the table and check my messages. I had to wait until I went upstairs to get ready for bed to see what I'd been expecting: another message from Ryan.

Are you ready?

"Ready for what?" I whispered.

That question kept me up most of the night, except for a nightmare about a new flavor of yogurt called Twinkie Toes. The next morning I was up before my alarm and already eating breakfast when my parents came down.

"What's this? Someone trying to get bonus points before Christmas?" Mom asked, kissing the top of my head. "Santa's making my boy punctual!"

"And sleep deprived," Dad said as I yawned wide enough to fit my cereal bowl in my mouth. "Don't fall asleep in class," he told me.

"I won't."

I fell asleep in the car.

Mom shook me awake, and I rubbed my face, leaning my head back against the seat.

"Do I have to go to school today?" I asked.

"Well, it's either that or work at one of the stores," said Mom.

I sat up. "Okay!"

"We need someone to clean up the goose poop by the doors," she added.

I picked up my book bag. "And I'm off to school!"

Mom smiled. "Bye, honey. Have a good day."

I smiled back, but in my head thought, *We'll see.*

Normally, my friends and I hang out in the school courtyard, but winter in Illinois can be brutal, and today was pretty cold, so our school also has a student lounge inside, which gets packed and *loud.* When I walked over to the couch where Brooke, Vanessa, and Heather were sitting, they didn't even look up. In fact, they were adding their voices to the chaos.

Brooke and Vanessa were facing each other

with arms crossed while Heather sat between them, twisting a pen between her fingers. They appeared to be engaged in a debate of the utmost importance.

"I'm not saying dolphins can't talk. I'm saying they don't have anything interesting to say!" exclaimed Brooke.

"Of course they do! They're very intelligent creatures, you know," said V.

"Hey, guys?" I asked. "Can you scoot over?"

They didn't hear me.

"Oh, they're intelligent?" Brooke raised an eyebrow. "What could they possibly know— which fish is the freshest? It's all fresh. They're in the ocean!" She threw her hands into the air.

"Hey, Heather, a little help here?" I glanced at her, but she got to her feet and turned to face Brooke and Vanessa. "Guys! Can you please stop fighting for one moment?"

Brooke and Vanessa quieted and looked up at

Heather. I inched toward the space she had left open, but she immediately sat back down. "Now, everyone knows whales have been talking—"

Instantly, she was drowned out by groans from Brooke and Vanessa, who jumped right back into their argument. I decided to take the opportunity to sprawl out on the couch. With my friends still on it.

All three girls shrieked and protested as I squashed them, finally forgetting their squabble and shifting to one side so I could sit down.

"Geez, you're heavy!" said Brooke. "What did you eat for breakfast, bricks?"

"Why are you guys arguing about dolphins?" I asked.

"V's trying to find the perfect gift for Gil," said Brooke.

Gil, as V had mentioned earlier, was her seventh-grade boyfriend. He worked at the newspaper with us as secondary photographer and the horoscope writer.

"Get him a crystal ball," I said. "Then maybe he can make some accurate predictions."

Vanessa gasped. "How dare you! Gil's horoscopes are always a little accurate every once in a while! Remember that week he said difficult times were ahead, and then the cafeteria ran out of curly fries?"

I stared at her. "Moving on . . . Where did the dolphins come in?"

"I bought this for him yesterday at the museum gift shop." Vanessa reached into her bag and pulled out a stuffed dolphin toy. "You know, because he was born in Hawaii." She squeezed its middle and it squeaked, "Help me!"

I cocked my head to one side. "Did that dolphin just say 'Help me'?"

V nodded. "Apparently, a lot of real ones are being killed by offshore oil drilling."

"Ah." I gave her a tight smile. "Well, nothing says happy holidays like cold-blooded murder."

"Ha!" Brooke pointed at Vanessa. "That's coming from a guy. Told you it was a bad idea."

Vanessa stuck her tongue out at Brooke and hugged the dolphin close.

"I thought it was sweet," said Heather.

"And I didn't say it was a bad idea," I corrected Brooke. "I just don't think it's the perfect holiday gift."

Vanessa put her other hand on her hip and looked from me to Brooke. "All right. Since you two are the experts, what *is* the perfect holiday gift?"

I scratched my head. "Gil's from Hawaii, right? How about a pineapple?"

"Ooh!" Brooke snapped her fingers. "A whole basket of Hawaiian treats! And maybe a CD of Hawaiian music."

Vanessa considered this, a wide grin appearing on her face. "That's actually not a bad idea, guys! I could even—"

"Uh-oh!" Heather was peering past V. "Gil's coming. Ditch the dolphin!"

V flung the toy aside.

"Help me!" it cried as it landed in a potted plant. Brooke and I snickered behind our hands.

"Hey, Gil!" Vanessa called as he approached.

"Hey, you." He hugged her when he got closer, waving to the rest of us. "What did you just throw away?" He squinted at the planter. "Is that a dolphin?"

"Of course not. They can't survive out of water, silly!" Vanessa laughed nervously. "Hey, look over there! Is that a light switch?" She took his hand and pulled him far, far away.

I turned to Brooke. "Since you're the gift whisperer, what are you getting Abel?"

Abel Hart was Brooke's boyfriend, a kid who

used to be in our grade but was so smart they bumped him up to seventh.

Brooke puffed out her chest. "The girlfriend gift to end all girlfriend gifts. A murder mystery train party."

I smiled. "Nothing says happy holidays like cold—"

She smacked my arm, and Heather laughed.

"In this case, it makes sense," Brooke informed me.

Abel had started a club called Young Sherlocks and was big into detective stuff. It's how he and Brooke met, which is nice, although now, Brooke tries to unravel any mystery she can find. Last week it was the mystery of who put melted chocolate in her gym bag.

It turned out to be her.

"Oh! Change the subject," Brooke said, pointing out Abel, who was walking toward us.

"Let me guess," Abel said with a smile, sidling

up next to Brooke. "Someone just asked who the most awesome guy in school was."

Brooke grinned. "I wouldn't give that secret up! One of these girls might try to steal you away!"

"Not a chance." Abel hugged her. "Besides, all the girls are gaga for Tim."

I smiled. Heather and Brooke groaned.

"Please don't tell him that!" said Heather.

"Yeah, now we have to spend all day lowering his self-esteem," added Brooke.

"I have great friends," I told Abel while the girls laughed.

"You also have a great watch," he said, staring at my wrist. "Seriously. I've been looking for something like that for spring training."

Abel was our school's track star. He had speed *and* endurance. Most runners have one or the other.

"Thanks! It's shockproof since I play so many

impact sports." I took off the watch so he could look at it. After studying it, he casually waved it under Brooke's nose.

"Pretty nice, huh?"

"Very subtle," she said as Abel handed it back to me. "But I've already bought your present. And it is so much better than any crummy watch."

"Thanks," I said.

Brooke nudged Heather. "What did you get Emmett?"

"Or do you even get him anything since you're Jewish and he's not?" I asked.

"Well, I'd get him a holiday gift, like I get all the people I'm close to," Heather said, turning pink. "But I'm not sure we're at that point yet. I mean, we haven't even gone on an official date!"

I nodded. "Just promise me you didn't get Stefan anything."

Stefan Marshall was our lead photographer

and sportswriter, who Heather had been crazy about since the start of school. At least . . . until recently when she learned he thought of her as a little sister.

Heather laughed. "The only thing he'll be getting from me is a smile."

"That's still too generous," teased Brooke.

The first bell rang, and the four of us headed into the hall. I scanned the crowd of students but didn't see Ryan among them. A few girls saw me and waved, but thankfully no one acted like anything was out of the ordinary.

What was Ryan waiting for?

I did a casual wander past the locker area. No Ryan.

I strolled by his homeroom. No Ryan.

I even went out of my way to hit the cafeteria. No Ryan.

The more I searched and the longer I waited,

the tenser I felt. In every one of my morning classes, I was poised for flight, as if Ryan might appear with my dance troupe and force me to frolic. When lunchtime finally came and my phone vibrated in my pocket, I yelped and jumped out of my chair.

Heather, Vanessa, and Brooke all stared at me.

"Sorry. Phone." I flashed it at them.

"Did you have it set to ants-in-pants?" asked Brooke.

I didn't answer, tilting my phone so they couldn't see it while I read.

It's almost time.

My jaws clenched. The cryptic messages were starting to wear thin.

Heather bumped my arm. "Everything okay?"

"Everything's great!" I said, putting on my best smile and leaning back in my chair. If Ryan was watching, there was no way I'd give him the satisfaction of seeing me sweat. "What are we talking about?" I asked, sticking my phone into my backpack.

"I've been thinking about V's gift for Gil," said Brooke. "We threw around some great ideas this morning, including my solution, which, I dare say, was brilliant." Brooke gazed modestly into the distance.

"Not to mention it was piggybacking on *my* idea," I said, rummaging through my stuff. "Also, calling yourself brilliant isn't a dare. A dare is . . . Eat this cookie I found in my backpack." I held up an Oreo riddled with pencil shavings.

Without hesitation, Brooke took it from me and popped it into her mouth.

"Ew!" shrieked Vanessa and Heather.

Brooke grinned at all of us with black-and-white teeth.

"Now, eat this penny!" I held up a coin, but

Heather forced my hand down.

"Don't do that. She'd eat a whole roll of them if you challenged her."

This was true. It was one of Brooke's biggest weaknesses, actually. She tended to bite off more than she could chew. Even if it was something covered in wood bits.

Brooke swallowed and ran her tongue over her teeth before continuing. "Anyway, our suggestions got me thinking. Mary Patrick wants us to do something special for the holiday issue, so in addition to our usual advice, why don't we offer holiday gift-giving advice?"

"What, you mean like post a list of gift ideas?" asked Vanessa.

"No, I mean kids who need help with gift ideas can put requests in the advice box, and we can provide suggestions. What do you think?" Brooke held her arms open. "It's only for a couple weeks."

"Sure," said Heather. "I'm always up for helping out."

"I don't know." I rubbed my chin. "Do we even know everyone well enough to do that? What if we suggest a jar of peanut butter and whoever gets the gift is allergic?"

"Who gives peanut butter as a gift?" Brooke asked, laughing. Then her expression turned serious. "That's what you're giving me, isn't it?"

"Not anymore," I assured her.

Brooke shook her head. "V, what do you think?"

"I think it's brilliant," she said. "We could put an end to gifted tacky Christmas sweaters!"

The three of them looked at me until I caved.

"Fine. At least I can make sure all my admirers don't get me the exact same thing."

Cue eye-rolls in three . . . two . . .

This time it was Heather's turn, but she did it with a smile.

"Just for that, I'm going to suggest 'giant pink teddy bear' to all your admirers," she said.

"And I will tell them 'giant pink teddy bear' is slang for 'gift card,'" I replied.

Brooke pounded the table with her fist. "Then it's settled! I'm off to the newsroom to clear this with Mrs. H and Mary Patrick."

Mrs. H, aka Mrs. Higginbotham, was our faculty adviser for the newspaper.

"I'll go with you," I said, picking up my lunch tray.

The less visibility I had to Ryan, the better.

Vanessa and Heather shrugged at each other and picked up their stuff too. Brooke zipped down the hall so fast I had to jog to keep up, while Heather and V lagged behind.

As soon as Brooke and I walked into the newsroom, Mary Patrick's hands went to her hips. "Where's this week's advice?" she asked. "It's due today!"

Every Friday we turned in pieces so they could be printed over the weekend for distribution the following Monday.

"The day isn't over yet," Brooke said, reaching into her bag.

"Why do you people always insist on waiting until the last minute?" asked Mary Patrick. "It's not like— Ooh! What's that?"

Brooke pulled a bag of Reese's peanut butter cups, Mary Patrick's favorite, out of her backpack. I could practically see the gold foil gleaming in Mary Patrick's eyes as the candy poured onto the desk.

She pounced on the bag and popped a piece into her mouth. "Tell me you guys came up with something special for the holiday issue."

"Actually," said Brooke, "we're not going to write something; we're going to *do* something."

She explained the idea for the gift request service and beamed at Mary Patrick. If Brooke was expecting a smile or applause or a tiny parade, she didn't get it.

Mary Patrick frowned. "I don't think gift requests are such a good idea. Giving general advice is one thing, but gifts are really personal."

"Told ya." I bumped Brooke's arm, but she ignored me.

"We'd be great at it!" she assured Mary Patrick. "Especially with the four of us contributing. We already helped Vanessa find something for Gil."

"Because you all know him," said Mary Patrick. "What happens if you make bad suggestions for people you *don't* know, and they have unhappy family members because of us? I can't have you ruining this paper's reputation. We've got a statewide newspaper contest next month!"

Brooke rolled her eyes. "It's not like we're going to recommend a flamethrower to someone's kid brother."

"Well, not if he already has one," I amended. Brooke shot me a look.

Mary Patrick shook her head. "Sorry, but you'll have to come up with something different. I can't have dozens of bad Christmases on my conscience."

I nodded. "That's okay, we'll—"

"Do it on our own, then," Brooke said, crossing her arms.

"We will?" I asked.

"Yes, and we'll show *you* that you're wrong." She pointed at Mary Patrick, who responded with a raised eyebrow. "Heck, maybe we'll start our own paper!" exclaimed Brooke.

"Whoa!" I held up both hands.

"Okay, maybe not that," she agreed. "But we'll give gift advice, and kids will love it!" Brooke hammered her fist into her palm.

Mary Patrick didn't back down. "Do whatever you want, as long as you don't bring the paper into it." Without waiting for an answer, she stormed off in one direction while Brooke stormed off in the other.

". . . doesn't think I can do it. I'll show her," Brooke muttered to herself.

"Are you sure going up against Mary Patrick is such a good idea?" I asked, following Brooke to our corner of the room.

"She's always acting like she knows what's best for this paper." Brooke dropped into her chair. "Someone needs to prove her wrong."

Heather and V joined us with the day's collection of advice requests to sort through.

Brooke picked one up and grinned triumphantly. "Ha! See? People are already asking for gift advice. In your face, Mary Patrick!" She patted herself on the back. "Good job, me."

Heather and Vanessa exchanged an amused look.

"Did we miss something?" asked Heather.

"We're going to war with Mary Patrick," I explained.

"Not actual war, right?" V asked, wrinkling her nose. "Because camo is last season."

"It's not war," Brooke said, pulling out her notebook. "War implies two sides are fighting."

Heather nodded. "Glad we're not—"

"This will be annihilation!" Brooke gave a slightly insane cackle.

"Taking this too far," Heather finished with a frown. "Why are we going to war exactly?"

Brooke was scribbling a mile a minute on her paper. "Mary Patrick didn't like the idea of us giving gift advice because she thinks we'll do a bad job. We're going to prove her wrong. And since she won't let us affiliate ourselves with the paper, we'll have to advertise in Locker 411."

She turned her notebook so the rest of us could read it.

Need a gift for your grandma?
Need a present for your parent?
Your esteemed advice columnists Brooke,
Heather, Tim, and Vanessa can help!
Drop a note in the advice box to tell us who
you're shopping for, and we'll do the rest!

"Not bad," said Heather, "but if we're not allowed to mention the paper, we probably shouldn't mention we're advice columnists. Or use the advice box."

"Good catch!" Brooke crossed out *your esteemed advice columnists* and changed *the advice box* to *Locker 411*. "V, will you make this look prettier?" She ripped out the page and handed it over.

The warning bell rang, and students began trickling into the classroom.

"Okay," said Brooke. "I know Mary Patrick's being a pain, but I really do need to know where you guys are on this week's advice."

"Finished," I said, handing over a sheet of notebook paper.

"Me too," Heather said, searching through her binder.

"Here's mine," said Vanessa. She pushed a paper across the desk while she finished coloring in the flyer.

"Aw, man!" Brooke collected them all. "I'm the last one again."

Her phone buzzed and rattled on the table. She frowned at the screen. "I got a new email from . . . I don't know who."

She held up the phone so we could all see.

The subject line simply said, "Twinkletoes." My stomach turned over.

Brooke clicked on the message. "Looks like someone sent me a video link. Should I open it?"

"No," I said in a horrified whisper.

But Brooke didn't hear me. A second later,

a tambourine rattled and a woman sang, "I feel pretty! Oh so pretty!"

"What . . ." Brooke's face broke into a grin, and she started to giggle. "Oh my God. You guys have to check this out." She held her phone up so we could all see.

Heather and Vanessa started laughing at the antics of the guy on-screen. He was prancing about in a billowy white skirt, white tights, and shoes with pompoms on the toes. His face was blurred out, but I knew instantly who it was.

Me.

CHAPTER

Going Viral

The video was slowed down and sped up in just the right places so it synced perfectly with the music. Dancing Me even paused in front of a studio mirror just as the woman sang, "See the pretty girl in that mirror there?"

My friends were practically doubled over with laughter.

I shrunk down a little in my chair. If I stayed quiet, maybe they wouldn't notice.

"I wish his face wasn't blurred out," said Brooke. "I wonder if he's singing along."

"Wait a minute." Vanessa plucked the phone from Brooke's hand.

Uh-oh.

"I've seen this outfit before." V paused the video and stared at the screen.

Leave it to our fashion expert to recognize my costume.

A second later, she gasped and looked at me. "You!"

"Shhh!" I put a hand over her mouth. "Nobody else knows."

"Knows what?" Heather asked, wrinkling her forehead.

"Hold up." Brooke took back her phone and gawked at the image. Then at me. "No way!"

"Oh!" Heather's eyes grew wide as realization sunk in. "Why did you post this video online where anyone could see it?"

"And someone clearly has, judging from that email," added Vanessa.

I gawked at both of them. "You really think—"

"Shhh!" Mary Patrick gave us a stern look.

I lowered my voice and my entire body closer to the desk. "You really think I'd post a video of myself dancing to 'I Feel Pretty'?"

Brooke let out a laugh but quickly stifled it when she saw the murderous look on my face. "Sorry. But you did look pretty."

Vanessa snorted and Heather looked away, but I could see the smile tugging at Heather's mouth.

"Congratulations," I said, scowling. "You've all gone from getting jars of peanut butter for Christmas to getting jars of *nothing*."

"Oh, come on." Brooke squeezed my arm. "You can't even tell who it is."

"If you didn't post it, do you know who did?" asked Heather.

The last thing I needed was my friends confronting Ryan and making things worse. The other guys in school would think I couldn't fight my own battles.

"No," I said. "But I hope no one else—"

I didn't even get a chance to voice my hope before it was dashed. From across the room, I heard . . .

"I feel pretty! Oh so pretty!"

Followed by . . .

"Ba ha, ha, ha!"

Everyone in class glanced over to where Stefan Marshall was sitting, one hand holding his phone, the other wiping tears of laughter from his eyes.

"Phone away before I take it away," Mrs. H warned him.

"But, Mrs. H, you gotta see this video someone just emailed me." Stefan held up his phone, and several people crowded around.

The laughter grew louder.

"Dude, send that to me," said Felix, a guy who

wrote for the front page.

The front page.

"Please no," I mumbled.

"Oh wait, never mind," said Felix. "I got it in my email too." He stared at the screen. "Aw, man! Looks like the whole school did. So much for a front-page scoop."

"What?" I started to stand, but Brooke immediately pulled me down.

"Be cool!" she whispered.

It didn't matter. Nobody was paying attention to me. Well, not the real me, anyway. They were too fixated on Dancing Me. Even Mary Patrick and Mrs. H.

Different snippets of "I Feel Pretty" filled the air, along with giggles and groans at my dance moves.

"What a dork!" someone said.

"Who is it?" someone else asked. "The email said it's someone at this school!"

"I'm sure he'll be easy to spot," said Stefan. "Just play this song and see who leaps down the hall."

Several people laughed.

"I actually like it," said Mrs. H. "If you take the music away, it's rather impressive."

"I think so too," spoke up Mary Patrick. Then her voice started to get louder. "WHOEVER THIS IS"—she glanced our way, and Vanessa gave the slightest shake of her head—"must have trained very hard," she finished in a softer voice.

"Yeah, and he's got some serious muscles," said another girl.

"I wish we could see his face." The girl in charge of the clubs section giggled. "I'll bet he's cute."

I should've been flattered and happy that at least I had some teacher and classmate support, but the guys wouldn't stop jeering and laughing at the video.

"Does the circus still accept runaways?" I muttered to my friends.

"We need to get to the bottom of who shared this," said Brooke. "It's got to be one of those sports goons who are always picking on you in gym."

Heather and Vanessa nodded their agreement.

"No." I shook my head. "No way. I don't want to draw attention to myself. If whoever did this finds out I'm on to him . . . or her," I hastily added, "they'll tell everyone the truth. I'll handle it myself."

Before Brooke could answer, Gil strolled over, grinning. "Did you guys see that video?"

A twinge of irritation sprung up inside me. Yeah, he didn't know it was me in the video, but he still shouldn't be laughing at someone just for dancing.

Then suddenly Brooke was laughing too.

"Ha, ha, ha! Lame, right? We all got a good laugh, didn't we?" She looked to the rest of us with an insistent smile.

Best way to go unnoticed: be one of the crowd.

I forced a laugh of my own. "Yep. And that music! You'd think he would've picked something better, like Beeth— OW!"

Underneath the desk someone stomped on my foot. Judging by the weight of it, I guessed it was Vanessa, who was wearing chunky boots.

She giggled up at Gil. "Hilarious!"

Heather smiled and said, "I know it's mean to laugh at someone who obviously takes his craft seriously, but the way it's presented is pretty funny."

Only my tenderhearted friend could make a jab sound like an apology.

My phone vibrated again.

Everyone's laughing about you. Fun, isn't it? Unless you want them laughing AT you, meet me under the clock in the main hall when the bell rings.

I squeezed my phone so hard I was afraid it might shatter.

Vanessa bumped my arm. "Right, Tim?"

I lowered my phone and looked up. "Huh?"

"I was saying the guy in this video probably doesn't really go to our school," she repeated.

"Oh." I nodded. "Yeah, I'm sure whoever sent this found it on the internet."

"I don't think so," chimed in Stefan. "It has an original posting date of twelve thirty p.m. today. That's a minute before I received it." He smiled. "Hey, I could be the first person in school to see a video that goes viral!"

Brooke held up a hand. "But I—"

"Yep!" I interrupted. "Stefan, you're the first. Congrats, bro."

"Thanks, man." He took a deep breath and sighed contentedly. "I should talk to Felix about getting this on the front page!" Stefan tapped Gil on the chest. "You can take my photo for it!"

The two of them walked off, and I relaxed my body. Brooke pointed to herself.

"But I was the first person to see the video."

"We know that." I gestured around the square of desks. "But if anyone else knew, they'd wonder why you didn't say anything, like Stefan did. They'd wonder if you were protecting whoever was in the video."

Brooke sighed. "Yeah, I see your point."

Heather bumped her. "Cheer up. Do you really want your fifteen minutes of fame to be that you were the first to see a silly dance video?" She widened her eyes and reached for my arm. "No offense."

It took several minutes for Mrs. H to regain control of the classroom, and when she finally did, it was agreed that the dance clip should get a mention in Monday's issue as part of a piece on how videos go viral.

Great.

After that, it was business as usual, with updates from the different sections and small group work. I must've had a look on my face that said I didn't want to talk because the girls all worked quietly on answering their advice questions.

When the bell rang I grabbed my bag and hurried out the door, making a beeline for the clock in the main hall. Ryan was already there, leaning against the wall with a cocky smirk on his punchable face.

"Well, well. If it isn't the video star," he said.

"Shh!" I ducked and looked around to see if anyone had heard. "How did you even get that footage, anyway?"

"My aunt and I were walking into the store

next to the dance building when I saw you going in. Or rather . . . running in with your bag by your head. You don't like people knowing you dance, do you?"

"It's none of their business," I said.

"I get that." Ryan reached into his back pocket. "So here's what's going to happen if you want it to stay none of their business."

He handed me a folded sheet of paper.

"What's this?" I unfolded it.

"Just a few tasks I need you to complete," said Ryan. "You know . . . if you want your identity to remain a secret. I still have the original, unblurred version of that video."

I stared at him, dumbfounded. "You're blackmailing me?"

He made a face. "Blackmail is such an ugly word. Let's call it . . . an agreement between friends."

"You're not my friend; you're disgusting." My

fists clenched, the paper he handed me crumpling in one of them.

"Oh, careful with that," he said, pointing to the list. "That's your only copy."

Taking a deep steadying breath, I unfolded it and read the contents:

Shovel my sidewalk
Clean my room
Do my homework
Get me into Berkeley's party
Get Lisa Wheeler to go out with me

I lowered the paper. "So basically I'm your servant," I said flatly.

"And matchmaker," he added, indicating the item about Lisa Wheeler.

"She'll never go out with you," I said, shaking my head. "You call her Lisa Wheezer, *and* she's out of your league."

Ryan pressed his lips together and took the list from me. Pulling out a pen, he scratched out the last task and scribbled something below it. "Fixed."

Make me the coolest guy in sixth grade

"I didn't put 'in the whole school' because I know there are some unbeatables," he said.

"How humble of you," I said, balling up the paper and shoving it into his chest. "But you can forget it."

Instead of responding, Ryan tapped the shoulder of a guy walking past with some of his buddies. When he stopped and turned, they all did.

I had a sinking feeling in my stomach.

"Tim, what's up?" The guy, Mitchell, gave me a nod, ignoring Ryan. I knew Mitchell from math class, although I hadn't expected him to know who *I* was. While I got a tiny flicker of joy from that fact, it was quickly snuffed out by the look on Ryan's face. Clearly, he didn't enjoy being ignored.

"Have you seen the video going around this afternoon?" Ryan asked the group.

Mitchell shook his head. "Video?"

Ryan pulled out his phone, video already loaded, and pressed play.

The guys all gathered to see and hear it better, and after a few seconds my performance was met with laughter once again. Heat surged into my face and ears.

"Know what's even funnier?" Ryan stared at me while they continued to watch. "It's someone at this school."

"For real?" One of the guys took Ryan's phone from him. "Who is this dork?"

More enemies. Yay.

Before he could answer, I cut in. "We haven't figured it out yet," I said.

Mitchell elbowed me. "If you do, let me know."

He sauntered away with his buddies, and Ryan handed me the crumpled chore list.

"Enjoy the rest of your afternoon. You can shovel the walk and clean my room tomorrow morning. I'll text you my address."

Without a word, I took the list.

At least it was short.

The warning bell rang, and both Ryan and I walked into our history classroom. Berkeley looked up and waved me over.

"Hey! Did you get my message about the party? Can you make it?"

"Yep," I said. "I'm there."

"Awesome." He gave me a thumbs-up. "I really want you to meet Alistair."

"Me?" I couldn't help smiling. "Really?"

"Yeah, dude. I think he'd like you. You're pretty cool."

I stood a little taller. "Thanks!"

He chuckled to himself. "The way you shut Ryan up? Awesome."

"Oh." My hands went into my pockets, the list of chores brushing against my fingertips. "Listen . . . about Ryan. I've been talking to the guy, and I think he's just misunderstood." I leaned closer. "You know, trying too hard just to get attention. He could really use some friends."

Berkeley winced. "Yikes. Good luck with that plan."

I pressed my lips together. "Actually, I was hoping you could help me. Do you think he could maybe come to your party?"

"Aw, dude, I don't know . . ."

"What if I promised he'd be on his best behavior?" I added. "I could spruce him up and teach him some manners."

Berkeley sighed and rubbed the back of his head. "Yeah, okay." He looked up at me. "But the second he gets annoying . . ."

"He won't," I promised, crossing my heart. "Thanks."

"Students, to your seats!" called Mr. E.

There was a commotion of shuffling and chairs sliding across the floor as everyone sat.

"Thanks again," I whispered to Berkeley, heading to my own desk. While Mr. E started the lesson, I pulled out the chore list and scratched off *Get me into Berkeley's party*.

One down, four to go.

CHAPTER

4

The Life of Ryan

Here's another thing about me. I want to be rich someday. Like . . . own-a-professional-sports-team rich. And not a team that's on a losing streak, sponsored by athlete's foot cream and prunes. I want three-time national champs sporting Under Armour and chugging Gatorade.

But you don't get rich doing someone else's chores for free.

Needless to say, I wasn't in the best mood Saturday morning when Mom dropped me off in front of Ryan's house.

"What's with the face?" she asked when she pulled to the curb.

I shrugged. "You and Dad gave it to me."

Mom raised an eyebrow. "That was rude. Want to try again?"

"Sorry," I said, unbuckling my seat belt. "I just don't want to do this group project."

It was the lie I'd come up with to explain why I was up so early on a weekend, spending time with someone my parents barely knew.

Mom cradled my cheek in one hand and kissed my forehead. "Don't worry. You'll only have to work with other people another"—she tilted her hand from side to side—"fifty years or so."

I smiled. "No way. In a couple years everything will be controlled by machines."

She patted my leg. "Dad and I really need to show you those Terminator movies. Have fun and call me when you're ready to go."

I waved to her and slung my completely

empty backpack over one shoulder as I stepped onto Ryan's snowy lawn. I immediately sank into powder all the way to the shins of my boots. Glancing at the houses on either side, both of which had only a few inches of snow, I had to wonder if Ryan had stockpiled the stuff just for me.

When I was halfway to his front door Ryan opened it, clad in a T-shirt, board shorts, and flip-flops.

"Right on time. I like that in an employee," he said.

"First of all, it's thirty-four degrees out." I pointed to the steam my breath was making. "You look like an idiot. Second, I'm not your employee. They get paid." I rubbed my thumb against my fingertips.

He blinked at me. "So the shovel is right there." He pointed to one that was leaning against the porch railing next to a bucket of salt. "I find it's best to do the walkway first before you get too tired."

"Yeah, yeah," I muttered, tossing my backpack onto the porch.

I picked up the shovel and cleaned off the steps as I went down each one. Ryan followed right behind with a lawn chair under one arm and a thermos in the other.

"Again, it's thirty—" I stopped myself, and gestured to him. "You know what? Freeze to death. That would be great for me."

Ryan unscrewed the lid of his thermos and poured himself some hot chocolate. "Nah. I want to enjoy this," he said, but I could see goose bumps on every visible inch of skin.

"Shouldn't you be sipping some slushy drink out of a coconut?" I asked as he settled back into his lawn chair.

He snorted. "Don't be ridiculous. It's thirty-four degrees out."

I shook my head, popped in my earbuds, and put on some music. I managed to shovel about two feet of the walkway before something cold and hard smacked into the side of my face.

"Ah!" I dropped the shovel and wiped at my cheek. Little pieces of snow trickled down. I spun and glared at Ryan. "What was that for?"

"I asked you a question and you didn't hear me," he said, wiping a hand on his board shorts. "And now my fingers are numb."

"Serves you right!" I said. "What do you want?"

"What are you listening to?" he asked.

I stared at him. "Are you seriously trying to make small talk while you're blackmailing me?"

Ryan shrugged. "I'm bored."

"So go inside and watch TV," I said, picking up the shovel. "I'm not here to chitchat. I'm here to cross items off your stupid list."

Ryan opened his mouth to respond but then

paused, tilting his head to one side, as if listening for something. His eyes widened, and he threw the contents of his cup on the snow. Then he recapped the thermos and scrambled out of his chair.

"Hand me the shovel," he said.

"What?" He didn't even wait for me to comply before yanking it out of my hand. "What are you doing?" I asked.

"Just shut up and sit in the lawn chair!" he said with such force that I was momentarily startled into sitting.

Snow started flying left and right from Ryan's shovel as he cleared the walkway. A moment later, a car appeared around the corner and pulled up the drive.

I watched in fascination as a stout woman in a waitress's uniform stepped out and scowled at Ryan.

"Hey, Aunt Sue!" Ryan said with a nervous

smile. "I thought you'd be at work all day."

"What on Earth are you doing in those clothes? You'll catch pneumonia!" She charged up the driveway toward him, and for a second, Ryan looked as if he might use the shovel as a shield.

But the woman paused when she saw me in the lawn chair. "Oh! You have company."

"Uh . . . yeah." I got to my feet and extended my hand. "Tim Antonides. Your nephew and I are working on a science project, actually."

I shouldn't have covered for Ryan; I should've let him squirm and suffer. Something told me, though, that Ryan and his aunt already had a pretty rocky relationship. I wasn't going to be the guy to make it worse.

"Antonides, did you say?" she asked, shaking my hand. "You can call me Sue." She looked from the lawn chair to her shivering nephew clutching the shovel. "What kind of science project is this?"

"Uh . . . ," I began.

"Thermodynamics," supplied Ryan.

I was surprised he even knew that word, and more important, that it was an excuse that made sense. Of course, I was also surprised he'd managed to create a humiliating video of me, so . . .

Sue nodded as if thermodynamics were the only thing it *could* be. "Well, have you done enough research? You're turning blue, and it's not a good color on you," she told Ryan.

He ducked his head and then mumbled, "Yes, Aunt Sue."

"In the house, then, both of you." She gripped one of his shoulders and turned him toward the door. "And hurry it up. I only came home to grab my badge. Can't waste time."

I hesitated for a moment before I followed, sighing deeply. Cleaning Ryan's room was on my list of chores, anyway.

"Did you offer your guest any snacks?" Sue

asked Ryan as we approached the kitchen. She grabbed a badge off the counter and clipped it to her shirt.

He shook his head. "I was going to, though," he said.

After he was done pelting me with snowballs. Sure.

Sue held an open cookie jar out to me. "I'm known for my prizewinning snickerdoodles."

"Thanks," I said, taking one.

Sue tossed one to Ryan and put the jar back. "All right, I'm leaving. Stay out of trouble." She pointed at Ryan and then walked back outside. Ryan's entire body relaxed, and he hurried to the peephole in the front door to watch her go.

I followed him and cleared my throat, holding up my blackmail list and a pencil. "So can we call that chore done or . . . ?"

He spun around, all serious and strong again. "It's done. Time for chore number two: clean my bedroom." He led the way back to the kitchen and opened a cabinet under the sink. "You'll need these," he said, pulling out a supply caddy.

I pocketed my list, on which I'd just scratched out my latest task, and studied the contents of the basket he handed to me. "Um . . . are these mousetraps?"

"Yeah, something's been eating the toast I keep on my nightstand."

"Why—" I shook my head. "Never mind. Any other wildlife I should be aware of? Should I set a bear trap or two?"

"Nope. Oh, but if you come across any spiders, add them to my spider jar." Ryan wandered into his living room and flopped down onto the couch.

I followed. "Spider jar?" I repeated, the hairs on my neck standing on end.

He nodded. "Yeah, jar. If they're in a box, they can get out easier."

"Uh . . ." I opened my mouth and then closed it, trudging upstairs. Below me I could hear him turn on the TV. "Even if I was getting paid, no amount of money would be worth this," I mumbled to myself.

And then I opened the door to his room.

"Whoa! No amount!" I cringed and backed away.

From the living room, I could hear Ryan chuckling.

Forget the supply caddy. The best way to clean this place would be to just burn it down and start over. I'd worn my boots to handle the snow, but I was grateful to have them on now as I stepped on fast-food wrappers and kicked a T-shirt aside. There was no telling what could've crawled up my pants leg.

"Do you have a laundry bag?" I called out the bedroom door. In a softer voice I added, "Or a blowtorch?"

I pulled on a pair of rubber gloves I'd found in the cleaning caddy and started gathering clothes into a pile, picking them up from the floor or lifting them off various items. The only thing he *hadn't* used as a clothes rack was his computer.

I dropped the shoe I was holding.

Ryan's computer.

When he'd filmed me with his phone, he'd no doubt transferred the video there so he could blur my face. That meant the copy showing my identity was on the hard drive! If I could access his computer, I could erase it and, if I was lucky, even remove it from his data cloud.

One step closer to regaining my freedom.

I tiptoed to his bedroom door and closed it, kicking a shirt underneath to jam it. Then I dropped the cleaning caddy and hurried to the computer, booting it up. The motor whirred and the login screen appeared.

"Shoot," I whispered.

His password could be almost anything, and I knew nothing about him. But there was also no way a kid who had an aunt like Sue could get away with total privacy.

I opened Ryan's desk drawer and rifled through the papers and pencils and random Skittles inside. Nothing.

I bent to pick up a paper that had fallen when I saw something taped to the side of his computer.

"Bingo," I said, straightening up. I typed in what I'd seen, and the computer finished its booting process. For just a second I paused to listen for any outside noises before searching through his recent files. "Aha!"

I completely cleared the file off his computer *and* data cloud (thank you, auto login!). Then, for good measure, I also changed the password on his computer before powering it down. All I had left to do was get his phone from him.

I waded back across the room, opened the

door, and called out, "Hey, Ryan? All your spiders got loose."

"What?" In less than a minute he was standing in the doorway. "What'd you do?"

His phone wasn't with him. Good sign.

I shrugged. "Sorry. I'll grab a second jar and some spider food. I think I saw a dead fly on the living room windowsill."

I strolled casually out the door, but as soon as I was around the corner, I raced down to the living room. Ryan's phone had been tossed aside on the couch.

"Please no password, please no password," I mumbled, picking it up.

As soon as I turned it on, I was in.

With a relieved sigh and a jackhammering heart, I clicked on his photo album.

There was the original video.

A fanfare played in my head as I deleted the video, followed by the roar of an imaginary crowd. I stood a little taller and threw back my shoulders.

Nobody messed with Tim Antonides and got away with it.

"Hey, Ryan? I've got some news for you!" I marched back to his room and found him sitting at his computer with a full jar of spiders.

"Geez!" I recoiled when he held them up.

"The spiders are all here," he said. "But my desk is a mess."

"That's because it's part of your room," I said.

Ryan placed the jar of spiders on the desk and swiveled in his chair to face me. "You must think I'm pretty stupid."

"That depends," I said. "What's the scale we're working with?"

He crossed his arms. "I sent the original video to my computer using email."

His email. It turned out I was the one who was pretty stupid.

I groaned and rubbed my forehead. "I didn't even think of that."

Ryan leaned forward. "And the password is only available up here." He tapped his skull. "You can't get rid of the video, and I can pull it up whenever I want."

I stepped toward him. "Look, Ryan . . ."

"I'm giving you a warning." He pointed at me. "But only because you kept me out of trouble with my aunt. If you ever mess with my stuff again, I'll make sure the original video goes not just to the school but to the entire world." Ryan got up and gestured to the desk chair. "Now reset my password and finish cleaning this room."

Without another word, he picked up his jar of spiders and left.

And I was right back where I'd started.

I worked straight through the morning and half the afternoon to get the room looking decent. Ryan saw it and grunted, but I took that to mean he was satisfied, so I crossed it off my list. Three down, two to go.

When I called Mom to pick me up, I asked her to bring a foot-long sub and a bottle of hand sanitizer. She didn't even ask why. I guess having a son who plays sports will do that to you.

While I waited I retrieved my backpack, and Ryan weighed it down with his homework.

"I'm really good at Spanish, so don't mess up," he said, passing me the bag.

"But I don't know any Spanish," I said, shrugging it onto my shoulders.

"You've got until Monday to learn," said Ryan. He turned me around and pushed me toward the door. "See ya!"

I stumbled forward and then glared back at him.

"Two more tasks," I muttered to myself, walking outside.

Mom pulled up a few minutes later and drove

in silence while I scarfed down half the sub before taking a break.

"How was the group project?" she asked, stopping at a light.

"Group project? More like group blahject," I said with a mouth full of food.

She stared at me. "Really?"

I covered my mouth. "Sorry."

"Group blahject?" she mused. "That's the best you can do?"

"Group . . . *poor*-ject?" I tried again.

She shook her head. "Your father would be so disappointed."

I grinned. "All right, you do better."

"Group project? More like group project . . . ile vomit," she shot back.

I almost choked on my food. "Gross! You've been working on that all afternoon, haven't you?"

"I've been batting some ideas around." Mom glanced down at my bag. "That looks a lot heavier than it did this morning. Like there's actually stuff in it this time."

I blushed and concentrated on my food. "It's just some books he's letting me borrow."

Mom patted my leg. "It's not a crime to hang out with one of the unpopular kids. You don't have to pretend."

I snorted. "Thanks. But . . . I don't think he and I will be hanging out again anytime soon."

"Why, he heard your group blahject pun?" she asked, making a face.

"Stop it!" I laughed and pushed her.

"Hey, I'm driving!" she said with a grin.

I settled back in my seat. "Mom?"

"What, sweetie?"

I looked up at her and smiled. "Nothing."

She smiled back. "I love you, too."

As soon as we made it home, I rushed upstairs and took a shower. Then I closed my bedroom room and settled down with Ryan's Spanish homework. I had just figured out that the Spanish word for *mosquito* was *mosquito* when there was a knock on my door, followed by the appearance of Gabby.

I covered Ryan's book with some of my own. "Hey, what's up?"

"Uncle Theo's here to take us to practice." She leaned against the doorframe. "Are you okay?"

"Sure," I said with a shrug. "Why wouldn't I be?"

Gabby stepped into my room and closed the door behind her. "Because of what happened at school yesterday."

"Oh, that," I scoffed. "You can't even tell it's me."

"Yeah," she said, "but someone was at the studio watching us. Someone from our school! Don't you want to know who it is?"

I shook my head. "If I did, I'd probably punch them."

"So it *does* bother you." She sat on the floor beside me.

"Of course it does," I said. "But it's already happened, and there's nothing I can do about it. And there's nothing *you* can do about it." I pointed my pencil at her.

She leaned back and put her hands up defensively. "Wasn't going to. But I did want to know how you planned to stop it from happening again."

My body went rigid. "You don't think . . ."

Gabby shrugged. "Whoever it is could make a whole series of videos about you."

There was another knock on my door, and Uncle Theo poked his head in. "You kids ready to go?"

All I could do was make a grunting noise.

"Tim's not feeling so great," said Gabby. "Would it be okay if we practiced without him?"

Uncle Theo's forehead wrinkled with concern. "Of course. Is there anything I can do?"

"I'll be okay," I told him. "I just need some rest."

He nodded and beckoned to Gabby. "Let's get going."

Gabby moved to follow him but paused at the door to tell me, "You need to figure out who sent the video."

"There's nothing to figure out. It's over and done with," I said.

But it wasn't.

Not only did I spend the rest of my weekend doing Ryan's homework, but on Monday *someone* had distributed the latest issue of the *Lincoln Log* in the student lounge. I walked into a sea of blurry-faced me, smack in the middle of the front page. I picked up a copy that had been tossed onto a chair.

"What Makes a Video Viral?" was the headline.

"Great," I muttered.

Berkeley was coming in behind me when he saw the paper.

"Dude, did you see that video?" He pointed to the page, grinning.

"Yeah," I said with a forced laugh. "Crazy, right?"

"No joke! I didn't think guys could kick that high."

"It's all about flexibility," I said. Berkeley gave me a curious look, and I stammered, "I—I mean . . . one would think."

He blinked at me. "Well, listen, I want to make sure you're still planning on . . . having Ryan presentable at my party." He cleared his throat. "I saw him in the bus line rolling a sheet of paper into a cone and burping in it."

"Of course," I promised. "When you see him

he'll be a completely different person."

"Cool," Berkeley said with a grin. "Hey, me and some of the other guys are heading outside to cover Mitchell with snow so he can pretend to be a snowman and scare people. Wanna come?"

Before I could answer, someone tapped me on the shoulder. "Excuse me. I saw you—"

"That's not me! I'm a terrible dancer!" I cried, spinning around.

A girl with messy hair and glasses jumped back, startled. "O-okay. I saw your ad in Locker 411 about gifts for your family?"

"Oh! Sorry!" I laughed nervously and glanced from her to Berkeley, who had raised an eyebrow. "Yeah, just put your request in the locker and—"

The girl shook her head. "You're standing in front of me. Can't I just talk to you?"

"Well . . ." I looked around for Brooke, Heather, or Vanessa, hoping to pawn her off on one of them, but before I could get their attention,

Berkeley clapped me on the shoulder.

"You do what you gotta do, Tim. I'll catch you later."

He trotted off, and I shouted, "Tell everyone I said hey!"

The girl was now shifting from foot to foot in front of me.

"Okay," I said with a sigh. "How can I help?"

"I need a gift for my sister," said the girl. "She doesn't like anything except chickens. Weird, right? I've already gotten her chicken pajamas and a Chicken Little hat—"

"How old is your sister?" I interrupted.

"Eighteen."

My eyebrows lifted. "Ah. Maybe start with slightly older gifts." I thought for a moment. "Have you ever thought about taking her to a farm to see them for herself?"

The girl's mouth dropped open, and her eyes lit up. "That's brilliant! When can you set that up?"

"Set what up?" I repeated.

"The farm visit, duh!" She smacked my arm.

Why are girls always hitting?

"I don't take care of that," I said.

She frowned. "But your flyer said if we tell you who we're shopping for, you'd take care of the rest."

I sucked air through my teeth. "Yeah, all that means is we'll give you gift advice."

"Ohhh." She reached down and rummaged through her purse. "Well, how much do I owe you for the advice, then?" I saw a flash of green, and for a moment I was tempted to name my price, but one of the rules of our advice column is that we can't profit from it. In fact, we have an actual rulebook with that written in it.

"There's no charge," I said. "Just happy to help."

"Thanks!" said the girl. "Have fun scaring people with your friends!"

As soon as she walked away, I headed for the exit, but another girl barred my path. "Did I just hear you tell that girl you're giving advice on gifts? I need help finding something for my boyfriend."

"Sure," I said with a shrug. "What—"

"Great!" The girl reached into her backpack and pulled out a clothing catalog with a billion sticky notes between the pages. "Because I'm torn between a few options."

"A few?" I asked, dropping into a chair.

She sat down next to me and turned to the first marked page. "What do you think of this shirt?"

I shrugged again. "It's good."

She squinted at me. "Good? Not great?"

"It's a shirt," I said. "No guy is ever going to be superexcited about a shirt, unless it's made of money."

The girl tapped her fingers on the catalog, then flipped ahead a few pages. "What about pants?"

The bell for homeroom couldn't come soon enough. When it did, and I was finally free of Catalog Girl (who decided to just go with a gift card), Ryan suddenly appeared by my side.

"And the hits just keep on coming," I said in a low voice.

"Relax," he said. "I'm not here to ruin your day."

"Then why *are* you here?" I asked.

"I need the details about Berkeley's party," he said. "When, where, how much food I can take home in my sleeves . . ."

"What are you, a magician? You shouldn't be putting *anything* up your sleeves." I grabbed him by the shoulders. "Look, I've been tasked with making you presentable at this party, so that starts now."

"Making me presentable?" Ryan's face darkened a little. "What's that supposed to mean?"

"It means all of this"—I gestured to his whole appearance—"needs work. Your clothes are wrinkled, your posture is prehistoric, and while shaggy hair is in, shaggy hair that looks like it's been chewed is not." I cleared my throat. "You're going to embarrass yourself at this party."

Ryan glanced down at himself and frowned at me. "Then you've got a lot of work to do, don't you?"

And I had plenty of incentive. A lot of people were talking about the video and watching it before morning classes, between morning classes . . . even in the bathroom. Unfortunately, the tile walls made the acoustics of the song even better.

Every snicker and joke about the video chipped away at me, so that by the time lunch rolled around, I felt about half my size. And I guess I looked it.

"Are you shrinking?" Brooke asked in the lunch line. Then her eyes lit up. "Or did I finally get my growth spurt?" She jumped and tried to touch the ceiling, but her fingertips missed by a mile. "Nope," she said with a sigh. "Nope, I didn't."

"You'd probably grow a little faster if you ate something besides pizza," I said.

"Pizza has cheese," she pointed out. "Cheese has calcium. I should be a friggin' giant by now."

"Calcium doesn't make your bones grow longer. It makes them grow stronger," I said.

She eyed me. "Then you must not be getting enough calcium, old man. But nice rhyme."

I pulled myself to my full height, and she nodded. "That's better. Now, I know what's bugging you, but sulking about it isn't going to change things."

"And what do you suggest I do instead?"

"Ignore it," she said.

"Ignore a problem and hope it goes away?" I shook my head. "That does not sound like the Brooke Jacobs philosophy."

"I didn't say ignore the problem," she corrected me, handing the lunch lady her meal card. "I'm saying ignore the reactions. By all means confront the problem." She pocketed her meal card and waited for me to pay. "Have you figured out who sent that mass email yet? I could deal with the whole thing for you."

There it was again. My friends to the rescue against someone I should've been able to handle on my own. I knew Brooke could probably destroy Ryan, but I also knew how much respect I'd lose from the guys if she did.

"No," I lied. "Looks like whoever it was just wanted a laugh from the school."

Brooke narrowed her eyes. "Nobody does something like that and chooses to stay anonymous. At some point, whoever posted that video is going to want recognition."

"Would you please let it go?" I asked, picking up my lunch tray. "I don't want to talk about it."

"You never want to talk about your private life," she said, following me to our usual table, where Vanessa and Heather were already eating.

"Because it's private!" I shot back. "Can we talk about something else? I've already gotten some requests for gift advice." I hesitated. "Well . . . sort of."

"Let me guess," spoke up V. "People thought you'd buy the gifts for them?"

I lifted my eyebrows. "Yeah, how'd you know?"

Heather and Vanessa laughed, and Brooke

covered her face with one hand while she dropped folded scraps of paper onto the table with the other.

"We found these in Locker 411," explained Heather. "At least five people got the same idea."

Brooke grinned sheepishly. "Yeah, I should've been more specific on the flyer. I'll make a new one, and tomorrow will go much better."

I picked up one of the notes that had a dollar stapled to it. "'Buy my brother something,'" I read and smirked. "So much love in that family."

Brooke elbowed Vanessa. "Watch it be from Gabby."

At that moment a belch echoed across the cafeteria.

I closed my eyes and sighed. I didn't even have to look to know who it was.

"Ryan is such a pig," Brooke said, making a disgusted face.

The other girls agreed and then started

helping Brooke come up with a new flyer. While they worked I stirred my mashed potatoes and watched Ryan scratch his neck with a french fry before dipping it in ketchup. Right before he put it into his mouth, he glanced in my direction and lowered the fry back onto his tray.

The kid definitely needed a serious overhaul.

I just hoped I had enough time to do it.

Manners Maketh Man

As much as it pained me to schedule Ryan into my life, I had to do it. Especially if I wanted to meet Adrenaline Dennis. While my friends and I sat in the newsroom, waiting for Journalism to start, I studied the calendar on my phone. All my time during the day was spent in classes, so I couldn't train Ryan then, and I couldn't skip my basketball games. *But* I could probably give up a few dance practices.

I sent two texts. One was to my uncle, saying I had to skip dance practice and asking him to pick me up from school later. The other was to Ryan, telling him to meet me in the student lounge after school so we could work on his manners.

I know about manners, Ryan texted back.

And you know about deodorant and toothpaste, but you never use them either, I texted back. If you want to be the coolest guy in the sixth grade, just be there.

The bell rang and I put my phone away, returning my attention to my friends, who were reviewing advice requests.

"What've we got this week?" I asked, picking one up.

"Boy wants to grow a beard," Brooke said, handing me a paper.

"Hmm. Girl wants to get rid of hers." I held up a different one.

"What?" Vanessa squawked, reaching for the request.

"I'm just kidding," I said with a grin. "She was actually wondering how to handle crazy static in her hair."

"Lotion," said V.

"Really? Won't that make her hair all greasy and flat?" asked Heather.

V shook her head. "Not if it's just a tiny amount."

"I'm gonna try that!" Heather said, reaching for her purse.

Mrs. H clapped her hands at the front of the room. "Good afternoon, students! It's time for Issues with the Issue!"

Issues with the Issue was something we did every Monday so we could make corrections and improve the next week's paper. Usually, it had to do with fact-checking the news or sports stats. Only once has the advice column ever been in it, and that was because of Ryan.

"This week's major issue," Mrs. H said,

holding up a paper, "has to do with the article on viral videos. Particularly the mention of Dancing Teen."

I was too surprised to be annoyed by the nickname. Someone actually had something to say in the defense of Danc . . . me?

"Wha—" I started to say, but Brooke elbowed me into silence.

"What's wrong with my article?" Felix asked.

Mrs. H held up a handwritten sheet of paper. "According to an anonymous tipster, you described this dance as a Russian *barynya* when it's actually a Greek *kalamatiano*."

I couldn't help smiling to myself. The anonymous tipster no doubt had the same handwriting as my sister.

"We'll need to mention that correction," Mrs. H continued. She moved on to a different piece, and soon, it was time to discuss content for the coming week's issue. Mary Patrick took over, marker poised on the whiteboard.

I sat on the edge of my seat, jiggling my leg a mile a minute while I waited for Mrs. H to call on the sports team. With Adrenaline Dennis going to Berkeley's house, I'd gotten an idea for a piece that might actually land me extra time with him *and* get me bumped up to lead sportswriter.

Finally, Mary Patrick turned away from the scribbles for each section and called, "Sports?"

Stefan Marshall leaned sideways in his desk, all confidence. "Adrenaline Dennis is coming to Berryville for a charity event."

I groaned and bowed my head. Leave it to Stefan.

When he was done talking, all eyes went to me.

"Tim?" pressed Mary Patrick. "What's your sports piece?"

"That was going to be it." I pointed to the board. "Adrenaline is coming to town."

"Not as catchy as Santa Claus," joked Brooke. At the look on my face she added, "Sorry."

"Do you have any other story leads, Tim?" asked Mrs. H. "Anyone else you care to interview?"

I thought for a moment about which sports were ending and which were beginning.

"Well, the track team starts practice right after the holidays," I said.

"Oh! You should talk to Abel," said Brooke. "He's hoping to break two different speed records, and he's been running 5Ks all fall to prepare."

I gestured to Brooke. "There's my idea. An interview with Abel Hart." I nodded to Brooke. "Thanks for that."

Mary Patrick wrote it on the board. "And, Lincoln's Letters, we're still waiting on an extra holiday piece from the advice column. In case you forgot while you were playing Santa." She turned and stared directly at Brooke, who stared right back.

"Santa doesn't give advice; he gives presents," said Brooke. "But I wouldn't expect people who get coal every year to know that."

"Oooh!" several people in class said. Others snickered.

"Yes, and how *is* that gift advice going?" Mary Patrick asked, crossing her arms.

"Just fine." Brooke gave her a confident smile. "We've had a few confused kids but tons of interest. You're gonna be sorry we're not mentioning the paper. It would've been great exposure."

Mrs. H cleared her throat. "Ladies, let's wrap this up."

Mary Patrick gave Brooke one last look of disdain and made a few comments about the tone of the next issue before we broke into our groups again.

"Wow, Mary Patrick is really against us

doing gift advice!" said Heather.

"That's because she doesn't know how good we are at it," said Brooke.

"We don't even know how good we are at it," I pointed out. "And we won't until after the holidays."

"Yeah, but people can at least tell us if they like our gift ideas." Brooke tore a piece of paper out of her notebook. "Which is why I came up with this survey that we can give people after we help them."

"Oh, this already feels like a bad idea," said V, reaching for it. Heather and I looked over her shoulder.

"'Question one,'" I read. "'On a scale of eight to ten, how satisfied were you with this gift idea?'" I glanced at Brooke. "Don't most scales start at one?"

"Not if you want to guarantee success," said Brooke.

"'Question two,'" read Heather. "'Aren't you glad this service was available?'" She frowned. "Seems a little one-sided."

Brooke shrugged and smiled.

"'Question three,'" read V. "'How do you feel about newspaper columnists who go above and beyond: great, really great, or outstanding?'" She lowered the survey sheet. "We are *not* handing these out."

"Not without a few corrections," said Heather.

I nodded. "You might as well forge a bunch of good ones if you're going to do something like this."

Brooke's eyes lit up.

"Don't even think about it," Heather said firmly.

"Fine, I'll fix it," Brooke said, heading for one of the computers on the side of the classroom. "You guys work on this week's advice."

While Mrs. H and Mary Patrick had been

talking, Vanessa had taken the time to sort our advice requests, which she handed to us now. Mine were the usual questions from girls trying to figure out guys, and a couple guys wondering how they could be more popular/cute/athletic.

"Why do girls want to know if guys miss them when they're not around?" I asked my friends.

"Because *we* miss *you*," said Vanessa.

"Awww, you do?" I teased.

Vanessa rolled her eyes. "Not you. Never you."

I clutched my hand to my chest. "Pain. Unspeakable pain."

"So what's the answer?" asked Heather.

"If we miss you, you won't even have to ask," I said. "You'll know because we'll make an excuse to talk to you."

She blushed. "Emmett does that sometimes."

Vanessa giggled and bumped against her. "Awww!"

Heather smiled and held up another paper. "I like this question from Faith Off. She and her friends are having a fight because it's the holidays and they believe in different things."

"You've got firsthand experience with that one," said Vanessa.

"Yeah, but I don't really feel it's a fighting point," Heather said with a shrug. "We should be free to believe whatever we want. The only thing we should all believe in is kindness." She uncapped her pen. "I'm going to put that."

Vanessa studied a request. "I wish the *Lincoln Log* was printed in color. This girl is asking about wintery colors that aren't the typical green and red."

"You could put it on the website," suggested Heather.

In addition to our print edition, the *Lincoln Log* also had a website, which allowed the advice column to help more people than we normally could in an article.

"Ooh, good point!" Vanessa said, setting it aside. "I'll save this one for that."

I'd already moved most of my advice requests to the website pile, and out of boredom, glanced through Heather's requests. One of them caught my eye.

Dear Lincoln's Letters,

Is it more important to be honest or to be liked? I keep getting invited to slumber parties, but I have to say no because I don't want anyone to find out I still use a night-light. I'm sad to miss spending time with my friends, but I'll be sadder if they think I'm a baby and stop talking to me. What should I do?

In the Dark

I nudged Heather. "Hey, do you mind if I work this question?"

She looked over the request and nodded. "That's a good one! Sure."

Brooke hurried past with a bulging folder. "Done!" She lowered her voice to a whisper, "And I'm putting these and our new flyer in Locker 411!"

Heather, Vanessa, and I exchanged amused glances, and Heather leaned closer.

"So, speaking of secrets," she started, tapping the advice request, "it looks like nobody's figured yours out yet."

I put on my most innocent expression. "Yeah, I've been really lucky so far," I said.

"You'd think whoever sent the video would want some recognition," V chimed in. "Especially after that article came out."

"Maybe." I picked up another advice request and waved it. "Hey, look, someone else who wrote the paper for gift advice! Do you think we can answer it?"

Heather shrugged but smiled mischievously. "It *did* come in through the advice box."

Vanessa giggled. "And we *can't* ignore our readers. What does it say?"

"She needs help with a gift for her mom who likes gardening and dogs," I told them.

"How about a paw print stepping-stone for her garden?" suggested Heather. "I'll bet they have a dog that could step in some clay."

"Good idea," I said, scribbling on the back of the note. "What about a second gift idea in case they *don't* have a dog?"

"One of those little indoor herb gardens," said V. "My mom has one, and even when it's snowing she can still get fresh oregano."

"Perfect," I said, jotting it down.

"Okay, I'm back!" Brooke dropped into her seat breathlessly. "What did I miss?"

"We snuck in some gift advice and talked about how lucky Tim's been that nobody's ID'd him in the video," said Heather.

Brooke narrowed her eyes. "Yeah, I've been

meaning to tell you"—she looked at me—"I've got a bad feeling." She turned to our other two friends. "I've been putting my Young Sherlock skills to work."

Her skills were at least a week behind, but I humored her with a nod. "Thanks for the heads-up."

"Now," she said, rubbing her hands together. "Let's answer some more requests!"

At the end of school I found Gabby and asked her to remind Uncle Theo to come back for me.

"You know he's not going to be happy about this," she said.

"I know, but I've got a project to work on. And school's the most important thing in my life."

"Yesterday you said pie was the most important thing in your life," Gabby said with a frown. "Right before you ate the last piece."

"I meant pi, the number we use in math," I

informed her. "Me eating blueberry pie at the time was just a coincidence."

"You're a terrible liar," she said with a smirk.

If only she knew.

I waited in the student lounge, hoping Ryan wouldn't show up, but a few minutes later, there was a burst of noise from the hallway as he opened the door and walked in.

"Let's make this quick," Ryan said. "I don't like being at school any longer than I have to."

"Fine," I said, approaching him. "We'll start with social skills. Lesson one." I held out my right hand, and Ryan recoiled.

"Did you pick your nose or something?" he asked.

I sighed. "No, that's something *you'd* do. I'm trying to shake your hand."

"Oh." Ryan reached out and shook it.

"Now, we try polite conversation," I said. "How's it going?"

"None of your business," he shot back.

I closed my eyes. "I'm not asking a personal question. I'm simply asking how you are."

"Oh," Ryan said again. "Let's start over."

I offered him my hand, and he shook it.

"How's it going?" I asked.

"Pretty good," he said.

Then we stared at each other.

"Now, you ask how I'm doing," I coached.

"But I don't care how you're doing," said Ryan.

"It's the polite thing to do," I said. "Even if you don't care."

Ryan rolled his eyes. "Fine. How are you doing?"

"Pretty good. Hungry, though. I hope they have good snacks here."

Ryan widened his eyes and glanced around. "There are snacks?"

"No, we're pretending to be at the party," I said, "where there will be snacks."

Ryan nodded. "Can we have snacks now, though?"

I was about to say something sarcastic but thought better of it. "Actually, that's not a bad idea."

Luckily, the student lounge happened to have both a drink machine and a snack machine. I bought two different types of soda and one bag of chips and carried them back to where Ryan was waiting.

"Here you go," I said, tossing him one of the soda cans.

Ryan made a face. "Grape? Gross!"

"Off to a great start," I said. "If someone offers you something you don't like . . ."

He studied the can like the answer might be printed next to the ingredients. Then he held it out to me. "No thank you?" he asked.

"He can be taught!" I said, taking the can from him. "Now—"

Ryan swiped the other drink and the chips from my hands. "Thanks!"

"Nooo," I said. "Those were mine, and I hadn't offered them to you."

"Well, that makes you a rude host, doesn't it?" he replied.

In response I snatched the soda back and after a brief struggle, the chips, too.

"I didn't want them anymore, anyway," he said with a disdainful sniff at the wrinkled bag. "They're all broken now."

"Better the chips than your nose," I mumbled.

"What?"

"Better be hip like the bros!" I said with a smile.

Ryan narrowed his eyes. "Anyway . . . what's next?"

I opened the chip bag. "Would you like some Doritos?"

Ryan peered in at the crumbled contents.

"You mean Dorito dust?"

I raised an eyebrow, but before I could say a word, he pasted on a smile.

"I mean, I'd love some."

I tried to pour them into his palm, but Ryan plunged his entire fist into the bag. When he tried to withdraw his hand, his sleeve got caught. Instead of gently freeing himself from the bag, Ryan shook his arm up and down, pieces of tortilla chip flying everywhere.

At least Berkeley's party would have entertainment.

After I cleaned up the snack debris, we tried more polite conversation.

"People love to talk about themselves," I said. "And they love to hear their own name. So ask them questions about their lives and try to use their name a lot."

Ryan nodded. "So, Tim, what's Tim's favorite sport, Tim?"

I frowned. "That might be overkill."

"Ryan is sorry," he said.

I closed my eyes. "Why are you using your own name?"

"Because you're right. I like the sound of it." He smiled.

By the time Uncle Theo came to pick me up, I kind of wanted to shake Ryan like a bag of Doritos. Our last lesson for the evening was how to accept and give compliments.

"I like your shirt," I told him. "Now you say something nice about me."

"You're smart to like this shirt," he replied.

I stared at him. "Try again."

Ryan squinted and rubbed his temples. "Hmmm."

"It is *not* that hard to come up with something nice about me," I told him.

Ryan snapped his fingers. "You're overly optimistic!"

I sighed and hung my head. I couldn't get out to the car fast enough.

"How was your project?" asked Uncle Theo.

"All I'm gonna say is that the payoff had better be worth it," I said, buckling myself into the backseat of his car. "How was practice?"

"We learned a new dance today!" Gabby said, glancing back at me from the front seat. "I think you'll pick it up pretty quick, though."

Uncle Theo nodded. "If we need to, we can stay a little longer at practice tomorrow."

I winced. "Actually, I have to work on this project again."

"Oh," said Uncle Theo. Then he fell silent.

"I don't like it either, believe me," I told him. "It's just going to take more work than I expected."

A lot more work. On Tuesday, Ryan seemed to have forgotten everything I'd taught him the day before, so I spent half an hour reviewing it . . . this time with imaginary chips. Then we sat in the media room and I made him watch a video of some of the classiest, sophisticated TV and movie characters I could think of.

"Look at the way James Bond moves," I said. "He's got confidence."

"He's got a watch that shoots laser beams," said Ryan. "What guy wouldn't be confident with something like that?"

"Okay, so pretend you're wearing that, then," I said, nudging Ryan to his feet. "And walk across the room."

Ryan stood and instantly dropped into a squat, arm held straight out in front of him.

"*What* are you doing?" I asked.

"My watch shoots laser beams," he said. "You really think I'm going to keep it close to my body?"

I groaned. "So why are you squatting?"

"A guy with a laser beam watch probably has enemies."

"So do guys *without* them." I gave him a pointed look.

On Wednesday afternoon, he remembered his basic manners, at least, but when I asked him to show up looking his best, he appeared in his regular school clothes with a bonus grease stain.

"Do you own any shirts with collars?" I asked.

"My pajama top," he said. "Do you want—"

"No." I pointed at his jeans. "How about any nice pants?"

"These are my nice pants," Ryan said.

"But you wrote on them." I studied a leg closer. "And drew half a bird sticking out of a cat's mouth."

"Inspired by real life," he informed me. "See, there was this chewed-up—"

I held out a hand. "Look at my face. Do I look like I want to hear more?" I had him sit in a chair. "Let's talk about reading people."

Ryan grinned confidently. "That'll be easy.

My aunt has a subscription."

I shook my head. "Not *People* the magazine." I pointed to him and me. "People. You need to watch how they react to your behavior."

"Why?"

"Because it'll keep you from getting punched." I opened my arms. "Talk to me like you usually would, and watch my face. What are you doing for Christmas?"

Ryan scowled.

"Okay, see, that topic clearly makes you unhappy." I gestured at his expression. "So I'll switch to something else."

But Ryan wasn't ready to. "Let me guess. You and your family are gonna sit around the tree, opening presents by the fire while you laugh and hug."

"Well," I said slowly, "we don't typically light the tree on fire. But yeah, we'll open presents and spend time together." I shrugged. "Just a normal family Christmas."

"Normal." Ryan's scowl deepened. "My aunt has to work on Christmas, so I spend the day by myself. Guess we're freaks, huh?"

I shook my head. "I didn't mean it like that."

"I usually get one or two presents. How many do you get?"

"Okay, now's the time to notice I'm uncomfortable." I pointed to myself. "Could we talk about something else please?"

"You brought it up," Ryan grumbled.

"And I wish I hadn't."

Still, my incident with Ryan stayed with me, and at lunch on Thursday, I asked my friends, "Are you guys thinking about how much a gift costs before you suggest it? Some people can't afford much."

Vanessa tilted her hand from side to side. "I'm

keeping it in Coach range."

I wrinkled my forehead. "What does that mean?"

"Not too cheap, but not too expensive," she explained. "Like a Coach wristlet."

"I'm also keeping it in Coach range," said Brooke.

At surprised looks from the rest of us, she grinned and said, "What I'd spend on a gift for my soccer coach."

We all groaned, and I threw a cracker at her. She caught it in one hand and crammed it into her mouth.

Heather hadn't spoken up yet, too intent on devouring the fried chicken she'd just sat down with.

"You know, nobody's going to steal that from you," I said as she gnawed a drumstick.

Heather blushed and held a hand in front of her mouth. "Sorry, but I skipped breakfast this morning to get to choir practice early. And I really can't function without pancakes, eggs, turkey bacon, fruit, potatoes . . ."

"How are you not the size of Santa Claus?" marveled Brooke.

Heather smirked at her. "Anyway, to answer your question, Tim, I've been suggesting DIY gifts."

"DIY . . . as in do-it-yourself?" asked Vanessa.

"Basically, homemade gifts," Heather said with a nod. "Like jars of cookie mix ingredients or candles or T-shirts."

"That's cool, but you're assuming the gift giver has the time and skill to make these things," I said. At the injured look from Heather, I added, "Not that they aren't great ideas! I'm just saying, not many guys I know are going to want to sit around and make candles or T-shirts."

"Yeah, I guess you're right," she said.

"And," I said, "you don't know how much

money they have to spend."

"Fine," said Brooke with a firm nod. "Every time we offer gift advice, we'll do it for three different price ranges: cheap—"

"Let's say *affordable*," interrupted Heather.

"Affordable," Brooke corrected herself, "average, and . . . What's a word for *expensive* that starts with *A*?"

"Aughhh!" I screamed. The others laughed.

"It's going to take longer to help people this way," V said between giggles.

"I know," said Brooke. "We'll just have to do the best we can."

But she didn't look superconfident.

And despite my efforts with Ryan, neither did he. While my friends and I ate, I saw him do his best James Bond swagger to a nearby table with his lunch tray, but his movements were wooden and stiff. When he sat he kept pushing hair out of his eyes while trying to lean casually on one elbow and eat a hamburger. At first, he started to stuff it into his mouth, but then thought better of it and cut it with a knife and fork. When he brought the fork up to his mouth, the bun, meat, and vegetables fell to pieces.

Normally, I would've laughed, but since my future rode on Ryan passing for cool, I cringed. Maybe he'd feel more confident inside if he looked better outside. Unfortunately, I'd already done what I could in that area.

But I was sitting across from someone who could do more.

When the bell rang to end lunch, and my friends and I were heading for Journalism, I held Vanessa back a second.

"Hey," I said, "I need a favor. Can you keep a secret?"

Jekyll & Hyde

I t's never a good start to a conversation when you have to restrain someone from throwing their shoe. But when V found out what I needed and why, instantly there was a small wedge heel in her hand and murder in her eyes.

"Where's that greasy little rodent?" she asked, scanning the cafeteria for Ryan.

"V, stop!" I pulled her arm down. "You can't hit him with your shoe."

She looked down at it. "You're right. He'll ruin it. I should've brought my old sneakers." Vanessa dropped her weaponized wedge and slid her foot back into it. "You need to go to Mrs. H . . . or the principal."

"I can't. And neither can you." I pointed at her. "You promised."

"That's before I knew what I was promising!" V pouted. "That was exactly how my brother, Terrell, got me to eat fuzzy cheese."

"Look, if you help me, I'll make it worth your time," I said. "How much do you charge for a male makeover?"

"I can't take your money," she said. Then her eyes brightened. "But I *can* 'accidentally' shave off Ryan's eyebrows!"

"No," I said.

"In that case it's twenty dollars."

I gave her a look, and she sighed.

"Fine. I'll do it for free because it's you. But Ryan's going to be a tough customer. Tougher than most. On top of his bad attitude, he looks like he styles his hair with bacon grease."

"I wouldn't put it past him," I said, remembering Ryan's bedroom.

We headed for Journalism, and I could see the wheels turning in V's brain.

"You know I can work miracles on the outside," she said, doing a full-body flourish, "but his insides need it too."

I nodded. "I've been teaching him manners and a little culture. When I'm done, he'll be oozing awesome from his pores."

"Gross." V wrinkled her nose.

I didn't mention that the goal was to make him the coolest guy in sixth grade. Otherwise Vanessa would never stop laughing. Instead in a quiet voice I said, "Remember, though. This is just between you and me."

That afternoon when Uncle Theo picked Gabby and me up for dance practice, he was surprised to find two other kids waiting with us.

"More dancers?" he asked, nodding at Ryan and Vanessa.

Ryan gave a loud, derisive laugh. "Not on your life."

Vanessa smacked him on the back of the head, all the while smiling at Uncle Theo. "We're working on a group project with Tim."

It was actually my idea. This way, Ryan could get his makeover and Vanessa could watch him to make sure he didn't sneak off to get more dance footage of me.

Uncle Theo raised an eyebrow at me. "But you have dance practice."

I nodded. "I'm still going. I just need to swing by the house first to pick up a few things. Is that okay?"

Uncle Theo nodded and held open the passenger door. "Let's get moving! We've got a lot to work on."

As he drove, Uncle Theo glanced at Ryan and Vanessa in the rearview mirror. "Vanessa I know," he said, "but I'm afraid I don't know your other friend."

"That's Ryan Durstwich," I said.

"Ryan Durstwich," said Uncle Theo with a smile. "It's nice to meet you."

"Thanks," Ryan mumbled.

The kid was confident when he was tormenting me, but scared of adults? Maybe I could just hire Uncle Theo to be my bodyguard.

We sped home, and I flung open the car door so Vanessa and I could jump out.

"Hurry!" Uncle Theo called after us. "The *hasapiko* won't dance itself!"

"Man, I wish he'd quit saying things like that," I mumbled as V and I rushed into the house. "What do you need from here exactly?"

"Everything," she said with a laugh. "You sprang this on me at the last minute, and I don't exactly have guy's grooming tools or clothes. Unless you want to put Ryan in my six-year-old brother's overalls."

I paused at the staircase. "Well . . ."

She grinned and elbowed me. "Come on, we have to hurry! The pico de gallo won't dance itself!"

We started in my bedroom, where V raided my closet and picked out a couple shirts. It made my skin crawl thinking of Ryan wearing my things, but I held open a duffel bag and she threw them in. She started for my dresser, but I grabbed her shoulder.

"I am *not* letting him wear my pants," I said.

"One pair," she coaxed, opening the drawer. "It's for the greater good."

"Fine," I grumbled. "But remind me to burn them later."

She nodded and shoved a pair of pants into the bag. "On to the bathroom!"

V darted off and I followed, but before I could even make it through the door, she dropped a handful of products into the duffel bag. I pawed through them and pulled out a stick of deodorant.

"Hey! He can't have this!"

She gave me a tight smile. "Yeahhh. You might change your mind after tonight."

"Gross." I dropped it and made a face. "This better be worth it."

The sound of a car horn honking carried up the stairs, and V tugged at my sleeve. "Okay, we're done! Let's go."

We were back in the car in less than two minutes, and Uncle Theo eyed the duffel bag. "Must be a big project," he said.

V nodded, glancing sideways at Ryan. "A massive undertaking."

Ryan scowled but stayed quiet.

When we got to the studio, Gabby held me

back for a second while the others headed for the door.

"You can fool Uncle Theo, but you can't fool me," she said. "What's really going on?"

I sighed. "I'm having Vanessa give Ryan a makeover so he can get into Berkeley Dennis's party."

My sister looked as if I'd just announced I was competing for Miss Universe.

"Why on Earth would you help him? He's a jerk!"

"Shh!" I started walking toward the building. "I'm just trying to do something nice, okay? It's the holidays."

She shook her head. "You're not telling me something. Normally, you don't want anyone to know you're a dancer, but it's okay for *him* to know it?" Gabby gestured at Ryan and made a disgusted face. "This isn't gonna end well."

"He won't say anything," I said. To myself I added, *As long as I do whatever he asks.* "He promised, since I agreed to help him."

Gabby studied me. "You know you can tell me anything, right?"

"If there was something to tell, I would," I lied.

When she realized she wasn't going to get anything else out of me, Gabby sighed and opened the door. "I just hope he isn't rude while we're dancing."

"He won't be," I assured her. "Vanessa will keep him busy."

As if to prove my point, V was walking around Ryan and jotting stuff in a notebook.

"You're taking an awful lot of notes," commented Ryan.

"There's an awful lot that needs work," she responded. V turned to me. "We're gonna need a complete overhaul on this one."

"Tim?" Gabby pointed at her watch. "We've

got to get changed and on the floor."

I nodded to her and told V, "Just do what you can."

"You got it," said Vanessa. "Where can I work my magic?"

"The storage room where we keep our equipment is pretty empty." I led the way down the hall and pushed open a door. "Sorry, it's kind of small."

Vanessa glanced at the ceiling and grimaced. "Not the best lighting either, but it'll do."

"Tim!" Gabby said in a more insistent voice.

I waved to V. "I'll see you guys later. Good luck!" I closed the door and hurried down the hall with Gabby.

"Do you think Vanessa's going to be okay in there with him?" she asked, looking over her shoulder.

I snorted. "Are you kidding? I think Ryan should be more afraid."

Gabby and I did a quick change in the bathrooms and joined the other dancers in the studio. We were a couple minutes late, but neither the choreographer nor Uncle Theo commented.

About two minutes into the first song, I saw a streak go past an interior window. When I turned, it was gone.

"Timotheos, focus!" Uncle Theo called. Everyone else was facing the opposite direction.

I turned just as something else rushed past. I didn't dare look back in case Uncle Theo called me out again, but I realized I could see the reflection of whatever was happening if I glanced in the mirror.

A couple seconds later, the streaks were back, and I could actually see what they were now.

Ryan was racing down the hall with a towel flapping around his neck while Vanessa chased him, yelling something I couldn't hear. I could see a comb in her hand.

I chuckled to myself and kept dancing. Ryan had wanted a makeover. . . .

A minute later he was dashing past again, this time with Vanessa right behind him, waving a pair of scissors.

"Uh-oh," I muttered.

Ryan reappeared from the opposite direction and stopped in front of the studio window. I could see his reflection in the mirror, waving his arms wildly to get our attention. Several of the dancers, who'd seen him too, stopped and turned to stare.

Vanessa had a pair of scissors poised over Ryan, but when she realized we were all watching, she tucked them behind her back and smiled.

"Tim . . . ," Uncle Theo said in a warning voice.

"Sorry," I said, dancing toward the door. "I told them to keep busy until I could join them."

I ran into the hall and closed the studio door behind me. "What the heck is going on?"

Ryan, wild-eyed, pointed at Vanessa. "She tried to kill me with a comb and scissors!"

"I was trying to cut his hair!" said Vanessa. "He needs to be made over from head to toe, and I was *not* going to start with those." She grimaced and pointed at his grubby sneakers.

"Where's your certificate from haircutting school?" Ryan demanded.

The two of them started yelling back and forth, getting so loud I was afraid everyone in the studio would hear them over the music.

I put my fingers in my mouth and whistled.

Vanessa covered her ears. "A simple 'Hey, V' would've worked."

"Sorry," I told her, turning to Ryan. "There's nobody I'd trust more with my hair than Vanessa. You're going to have to be okay with change if you want to be the coolest guy in sixth grade."

"Ha!" Vanessa quickly clamped a hand over her mouth when Ryan glared at her. "I mean, of course you can be." She held up her scissors and snipped the air with them. "But that starts with a haircut. And then we move on to the eyebrows." She produced a pair of tweezers from her pocket.

Ryan gave me a horrified look, and I shrugged. "You gotta do what the makeover guru says."

I walked back into the studio, but inside I was doing a high-kicking happy dance.

I jumped into the routine as if nothing had happened, and thankfully, neither Vanessa nor Ryan appeared in the window again. But when class was over, Uncle Theo pulled me aside.

"Is everything okay? You've been very distracted the last week or so."

I nodded. "There's just so much to do before the holidays. Last-minute projects . . . you know."

"Well, please try to focus. Remember, we've got a dress rehearsal coming up."

"I'll be ready," I promised.

He and the others went to change, and I

sneaked down the hall to check on Vanessa and Ryan.

"How's it going in there?" I asked, knocking on the door.

Vanessa poked her head outside, hair even more askew than normal, but her eyes were shining, even with a huge bump on her cheek.

"Don't tell me Ryan did that," I said, pointing.

She shook her head. "I was trying to calm him by juggling some lipsticks, and then I accidentally tripped over a chair. *But* I think you're going to be impressed with the final results."

I crossed my arms. "I hope so."

Vanessa stepped into the hall, being careful to conceal Ryan, and did a drumroll against her legs. "I present to you the new and improved Ryan . . . uh. . . What's His Face!"

She opened the door and gestured to it with a flourish.

Ryan stepped out in a pair of my pants, a

button-down shirt, and a tie. His hair had been trimmed and spiked a bit, and he moved with confidence, leaning against the wall like a *GQ* cover model. I hated to admit it, but Ryan could pass for good-looking.

"V," I said. "You should win an award."

Vanessa giggled and hugged herself. "It was actually pretty fun once we came to an understanding." She bumped Ryan with her hip.

Alarms immediately went off in my head. Earlier V had wanted to kill him with her shoe, and now they were acting like best buddies.

"What exactly did you guys talk about in there?" I asked, looking directly at Ryan. "And by that, I mean 'how did you brainwash my friend?'"

"Oh stop!" Vanessa pushed me. "Ryan's actually a nice guy. He apologized for everything and was really open to change once we got started."

He smirked at her, but the way he did it was almost smooth. Not his normal jerky sneer. "I have to admit, you were right about the eye-brows." He reached up and groomed one with the tip of his finger. "Well, done, V."

I cocked my head to one side.

They were on a nickname basis?

Vanessa beamed and bounced on the balls of her feet. "Show Tim the etiquette stuff I taught you."

Ryan leaned forward and extended his hand to me with an easy smile. "Ryan Durstwich. Thrilled to meet you."

"Uh . . ." I shook his hand. "You, too."

"That's an impressive grip you've got. Reminds me of this wrestler I saw—"

"Nope." Vanessa cut him off. "*Wrestlers* are not in a gentleman's vocabulary."

Ryan cleared his throat and tried again. "So what do you do for fun around here?"

Now I'd get him.

"I dance," I said, gesturing to my clothes.

"Wearing this. Pretty funny, right?" I even spun so my fustanella fanned out.

I expected Ryan to snicker or say something snide, but instead he applauded. "That's amazing! I wish I had that kind of talent." He clapped me on the shoulder. "Great to meet you."

He looked to V for approval. "How was that? Am I a classy guy or what?"

Never mind that I was the one who taught him all of it.

"Close," she said with a grin. "But you never bothered to get Tim's name."

"Oh man!" Ryan smacked himself on the forehead and chuckled. "I'm such a goofball."

Vanessa laughed too. "I'll be right back. After sitting in a closet for an hour, I really have to pee!"

She hurried away, and Ryan turned to study his reflection in the studio window. "Man, I look good."

"You sure do," I agreed, holding up the task list. "With personality to match! The coolest guy in the sixth grade, I'd say. Right?"

Ryan looked away from his reflection long enough to nod, and I punched the air triumphantly, crossing off the last item.

He turned to face me. "Except . . ."

I froze, eyebrow raised. "Yeah?"

"I've kind of gotten used to our arrangement." Ryan stepped away from the window. "I find it suits me. And I still keep getting hints of attitude from you."

My eyes narrowed. "What are you trying to say?"

"That we're not finished." Ryan bent to pick up his jeans and pulled out a folded piece of paper. "Here are your next tasks. If you don't do them, I'll reveal your dark, embarrassing dance secret, along with a new one . . ." He stepped closer and smiled. "That you're so weak, you let me blackmail you."

"You . . ." Words failed me, and I stared at him, openmouthed. Ryan slipped the paper into my vest pocket and patted me on the cheek.

"Don't just stand there, Antonides. You've got work to do."

The Truth About Tim

"You can't do that!" I exploded. "We had a deal."

Ryan studied his nails, unconcerned. "And I'm changing it. I don't see why you're freaking out. Have you even seen the tasks?" He took the paper back from me and pointed to an item. "Look: iron my pants. I only have one pair, *your* pair, so that's an easy one." He smiled reassuringly.

I stared at him, dumbfounded. "Why are you torturing me? There's nothing I've ever done to you that deserves this."

Ryan's smug expression slid into a scowl. "How about every time you strut down the hall like you own the school? Or how all the girls flock around you and ignore everyone else? Or all your family members who think you're so perfect?" He practically spat the words. "And with all that, you *still* have to make the coolest kids in class laugh at me?"

"Geez, let it go!" I threw my hands in the air. "You were being a jerk. You deserved it."

Ryan's calm demeanor returned. "And you deserve this." He waved the paper in my face. "This is for all the ordinary kids like me who never get justice."

I shook my head. "No. Forget it. This time I'm—"

"Timmy, let me paint a picture for you," said Ryan, leaning against the wall with his arms crossed. "You're in sixth grade now. You've still got two more years at Abraham Lincoln Middle

School. If I reveal your dance video *and* the fact that you can be blackmailed, how well do you think the next few years are going to go?"

I clenched my jaw but didn't say anything. The kid was an evil genius.

"Let me help you see it," he continued. "Because of the video, you'll lose all your admirers. Because of the blackmail, you'll be running favors for anyone who can dig up dirt on you. Your best bet is to keep working for me." Ryan placed a hand on his heart. "I will personally guarantee things don't get worse for you than this."

There haven't been many times I've wanted to cry. The last occasion, four years ago, was after my aunt Rose, Uncle Theo's wife, had died, and it was more out of sadness for Uncle Theo. Right now, though, I had to fight back tears of fear, frustration, and rage.

Ryan had complete control of my life.

All the mocking images came back again, complete with laugh track, until Gabby's voice busted through.

"Whoa! That's not . . ." She approached us, V grinning beside her. "Ryan Durstwich?" She reached out and tentatively poked him in the shoulder.

Ryan gave a chuckle that sounded friendly enough, but to me should've included flames and him holding a pitchfork. "Impressed?" he asked.

"Uh . . . yeah!" Gabby turned to Vanessa. "You did all this?"

Vanessa giggled and blushed. "Well, I didn't do *that* much."

"Don't be modest," said Ryan. "I was a mess; I'll admit it." He checked his phone. "But I should be getting home."

I snorted. "Like anybody there misses you."

Vanessa and Gabby stared at me.

"Tim! That was really mean!" said V.

"What's gotten into you lately?" asked Gabby.

Ryan placed a hand on both of their shoulders. "It's fine," he said, smiling at them. But when he looked my way, there was murder in his eyes. "I'm sure he'll make it up to me."

"Well, let me just grab Uncle Theo," said Gabby.

"I'll do it," I said. I had no desire to be around Ryan any longer than necessary.

Gabby didn't seem to mind. In fact, she vaguely nodded and went back to marveling over Ryan.

I caught up with Uncle Theo, who was talking to a couple of the female dancers, and when he saw me, he excused himself and hurried over.

"Is everything all right?" he asked. "You look like you've seen a ghost."

Yeah, the Ghost of Poor Choices Past.

"It's fine," I said. "Is it okay if we leave soon, though? My classmates need to get home."

"Of course," said Uncle Theo. "Just let me grab my things."

He disappeared for a moment, and the dancers he'd been talking with walked over.

"Your uncle has been telling us what a sensation you are!" one of them said. "And we have to agree."

"It's a pleasure to watch you dance," the other chimed in.

My insides warmed a little, and I couldn't help grinning. "Really? Thanks!" After being mocked for my dancing, it was nice to hear something good for a change.

"Are you excited for the upcoming performance?" one of them asked.

I found myself nodding without a moment's hesitation. "Actually, yeah," I said. "The Museum of Science and Industry is one of my favorite places, and to get to be part of their production is kind of awesome."

"I feel the same way," said one of the women. "I suppose I should practice my *divaratikos* some more."

"Oh, are you doing a special solo dance?" I asked.

The women exchanged a quizzical look before one of them said, "No, it's part of the group's routine. We were just doing it a little earlier?"

The other one snapped her fingers. "It was when you stepped out of the room."

"Oh," I said. "I guess I need to catch up on that."

Uncle Theo hustled over with a bag on one shoulder, but before I could ask him about the routine, he was scooting me toward the exit. "We have to go, Timotheos! I'm late for my date!"

"Another one?" I marveled.

My tone wasn't lost on him. Uncle Theo raised an eyebrow.

"I mean . . . another one! Good for you!" I gave

him a thumbs-up, and he chuckled. Then he put me in a headlock and tousled my hair.

"You may not realize it, but your uncle is quite the ladies' man," he informed me while I struggled to get free.

"Stop! Stop!" I cried.

"The noogie?" He let go, and I grinned.

"No, calling yourself a ladies' man!"

I dashed away before he could catch me, laughing until I reached Vanessa, Gabby . . . and Ryan. My feet slowed and my smile flattened out.

"Uncle Theo's right behind me," I informed everyone.

"So we heard," Gabby said with a smirk.

It was a quiet car ride home . . . for me, anyway. Uncle Theo laughed as Vanessa, Gabby, and Ryan told him stories about crazy things that happened at school, none of which involved me being a dancer. I wondered how Uncle Theo would've felt if he knew how much Ryan made fun of what we did. As soon as Ryan got out of the car at his house, it was like a poison cloud lifted. Suddenly, the air felt lighter and I could relax and breathe again.

After we dropped V off and it was just family in the car, Uncle Theo glanced at me in the rearview mirror.

"That's a very interesting class you're taking," he said. "Where the group project is to give someone a makeover."

I didn't even bother to act guilty. "That wasn't for a group project. Ryan just has a habit of getting what he wants." I hammered a fist into the seat beside me.

"Well, he should do that on his own time," Uncle Theo said with a disapproving tone. "He interrupted dance practice, and we barely have any time left before dress rehearsal. And *you* don't have all the dance moves down."

I sighed and leaned my head back. "I know."

"I can help him," Gabby said from the front seat. "I can teach Tim the moves he's been missing." She turned to look back at me. "Do you want to start tonight?"

I shook my head. "I have to do Ry— I mean, *my* homework." I shifted in my seat, and the square of folded paper that listed my new tasks shifted in my pocket, reminding me of its presence. Like I could ever forget.

Uncle Theo dropped us off at the curb and sped away to meet his date while Gabby skipped up the walkway ahead of me.

"What did you think of the new Ryan?" she asked. "Pretty dreamy, right?"

"More like nightmare-y," I said under my breath.

"What?" Gabby waited for me to catch up.

"I said V did a good job." I forced a smile.

"Do you think Ryan has a girlfriend?"

I almost tripped. "Oh no. You are *not* going

out with him. He may seem charming, but it's all an act. Trust me."

Gabby scoffed. "Like you can tell me who to date. Besides, I was just asking."

"He doesn't have a girlfriend," I said. "It would've made the news, along with all the flying pigs."

She rolled her eyes and opened the front door. "I think he cleans up pretty nice."

"Yeah, and you also tried to drown a guy in grape snow-cone syrup," I reminded her. "So excuse me if I don't entirely trust your judgment."

Gabby looked at me for a second and then shouted, "Mom? Who has better judgment, me or Tim?"

From somewhere in the kitchen there was laughter.

I smirked at her and shrugged as if to say *See?*

Gabby stuck out her tongue and headed to the kitchen, where Mom and Dad were studying a cookbook together.

"Why don't you think I have better judgment?" my sister demanded.

"Oh, that was a serious question?" Mom blinked. "I think it depends on the situation. Sometimes you both have great judgment, and sometimes you both have terrible judgment."

"Hey!" I sat on a kitchen stool. "Name one time—"

"When you were six, you wanted to be one of King Arthur's knights," said Dad, snapping the cookbook shut, "so you tried to saw off the corners of our dinner table to make it round."

"When you were ten, you thought it would be cool to build your own robot, so you hotglued the toaster to a skateboard," added Mom.

Gabby giggled. "I remember that. You called it the BagelBot 5000."

I pointed to each of my family members. "And you would have all been thanking me when BB brought you warm, toasty bagels in bed."

"After it learned to open the fridge," said Dad.

"And put bagels in itself," added Gabby.

"And go up the stairs," Mom chimed in.

I wagged my finger at them. "See, this kind of doubt is why the BagelBot 5000 will never be a reality."

Gabby wrapped her arms around one of Dad's. "So, what's for dinner?"

"I couldn't find anything quick in here." He held up the cookbook.

"Why don't we do a family scramble?" suggested Mom.

"Yeah!" said Gabby and I.

Family scramble is a group effort at dinner, where we start with a pot of linguine and each get to add one ingredient . . . within reason. My folks insist that the end result still be edible, so lemonade, marshmallows, and bananas are not allowed (all failed attempts by Gabby and me).

Dad rubbed his hands together. "Let me get the water boiling while you guys grab some ingredients."

Mom held open the pantry door and grabbed a box of linguine for the base. Gabby and I scanned the contents of the rest of the pantry for our scramble items.

"Black olives," I said, grabbing a can.

"Very nice," said Mom. "I'll go for some stewed tomatoes." She grabbed a different can.

"Cheese!" said Gabby.

Mom pointed to the refrigerator, closing the pantry door.

Gabby pulled out a bag of shredded mozzarella, and we placed all our ingredients on the counter. Dad studied them and reached for a potted plant by the sink.

"And I will contribute some fresh basil," he

said, plucking off a few leaves.

While we waited for the water to boil, I nudged Mom.

"So you have examples of my bad judgment," I said. "What about my good judgment?"

She regarded me for a moment and smiled. "Your good judgment comes in making decisions based on who you are," she said. "I've never met a kid who was more confident about the things he liked."

"Both of you," added Dad.

Gabby beamed, but I pressed my lips together and stared up at Mom.

"You really think that?" I asked.

"I really do," she said, hugging me close and kissing the top of my head. "If there's one thing I can say with confidence, it's that I raised two great kids who know who they are."

Dad cleared his throat. "And I was just in the background waving pompoms?"

"Of course not!" Mom let me go and reached for Dad, making kissy lips. Gabby and I both gave cries of protest.

"Don't do it!"

"Not near the food!"

But our parents ignored us and kissed anyway.

When I climbed into bed later, there were several voices in my head, and none of them belonged to me. I could hear Ryan's taunting, the two ladies at the dance studio praising me, and Mom telling me how proud she was that I knew myself.

Mom's voice spoke loudest.

She was right; I wasn't the kind of kid who gave in to a bully's demands. I never let people push me around. Why was I letting Ryan?

Because he could destroy me.

I flipped over in bed and punched my pillow. I couldn't let Ryan keep bossing me around, but I couldn't let him make me a laughingstock, either. I needed to stand my ground.

The question was how.

No answers came in my dreams, but for the first time in days I had a solid night's sleep. I knew who I was and who I *didn't* want to be.

I could figure the rest out in the morning.

"Running's easy. It's running fast that's the hard part." Abel Hart was sitting on a couch in the student lounge before school the next morning, talking while I scribbled in my notebook.

"That's good," I said, tapping the page. "Say more stuff like that."

He grinned. "You want me to spout inspirational quotes?" He struck a regal pose. "Life is full of hurdles. Jump or eat asphalt."

I snorted and scribbled out what I'd started to write. "Okay, let's just get to the important stuff. Brooke says you're going to break a bunch of records this season."

"Well, I'm going to try," said Abel. "I've never really been good at anything athletic except running, so I figure I might as well be the best at what I can."

"I like that," I said. "And how are you getting ready?"

"I swim in a kiddie pool of pudding. Builds resistance."

I gaped at him. "Seriously?"

"No!" He laughed. "I run! How else can you get good at it?"

I laughed too. "I meant do you eat certain things or have any rituals?"

Abel nodded. "I eat pickles. Lots of pickles."

"Really?" I jotted that down. "How do pickles help you run better?"

"Oh. They don't. I just like them."

I shot him a withering look. "They're never going to make a heart-warming sports movie about you."

He snapped his fingers. "I do always wear the same pair of socks before a race. Never been washed." He wrinkled his nose. "At this point, they could probably move without me in them."

I mirrored his expression. "Brooke sure picked the right guy. She also mentioned that you've been running a bunch of 5Ks. Is that . . ." I paused when I realized Abel wasn't paying attention. He was squinting at something beyond me. I glanced over my shoulder and fought back a groan.

Ryan was swaggering into the student lounge in *my* pants and a polo shirt that looked brand-new. Students around him were whispering and staring, but the looks they were giving him were ones of surprise and approval.

"Is that Ryan Durstwich?" asked Abel. "He's changed."

"Yeah," I said. "So about those 5Ks—"

"He's changed a *lot*. Kinda weird for that to happen overnight," said Abel, watching Ryan work the crowd. "And his personality seems almost tolerable."

"I guess," I said.

As if he could feel us staring, Ryan glanced over and gave us a finger point and a smirk. Abel continued to stare in fascination.

"Why did this happen?" he asked.

"He brushed his hair and put on some clean clothes."

Abel shook his head. "Not how. Why? People don't make sudden changes like this for no reason."

I shrugged. "I guess we'll never know. Can we go back to the interview questions?"

But it was too late. Ryan was headed our way.

"Hey, guys!" he said. "Tim, I need help with something."

"I'm kind of in the middle of an interview," I said, "but you can send in an advice request and maybe get an answer that way."

Ryan didn't take the hint. "It's about Berkeley's party and what to wear." He winked at Abel. "Gotta make a good impression, you know what I mean?"

I sighed and put down my notepad. "What you have on is fine, but if you're not sure, ask Vanessa. Now, if you'll excuse me." I gestured at Abel and gave Ryan a pointed look.

He looked a little taken aback but replaced it quickly with an easy smile. "Sure thing. I'll catch up with you later, dude." Ryan gave Abel a quick nod and walked off to talk to a group of girls who'd been huddled together, watching him. A second later they giggled way too hard at something he said. Now I knew how Brooke, Heather, and V felt when they watched *me*.

"What do you say we get back to this interview?" asked Abel.

"Good idea," I said.

I asked him a few more questions and, just in case I needed it, took his picture with my phone. "I'm sure Stefan and Gil will find all kinds of things wrong with this," I mumbled, pocketing my phone. "Well," I said, offering my hand to Abel, "thanks for meeting with me. The piece isn't due until tomorrow, so if you think of anything else . . ."

Abel held up a finger. "Actually, there's one more thing I'd like to say."

"Oh! Fire away," I said, pen poised over my paper.

He leaned toward me. "I don't think you should let Ryan Durstwich blackmail you anymore."

One Good Turn

Statues.

That's what Abel and I could've been. He sat motionless, elbows on his knees, watching me while I stared at him, openmouthed, pen still pressed to the page.

Abel squinted and pointed at my stupefied expression. "Tell me this isn't the look that gets the girls."

Out of the millions of words I'd read in books, only three came to mind. "You... How... Who?"

Luckily, Abel was fluent in Gibberish.

"Yes, I know," he said. "I've known since the

first time I saw you talking in the hall with him."

Abel got to his feet and started pacing in front of me in slow, methodical steps. "You're not friends, yet you spend a lot of time together. Your personalities have swapped. He's confident and you don't seem as much so. And now he didn't just ask for your help . . . he expected it. Clearly, he has the upper hand, which is saying something since Ryan's the kid who looks like he plays poker with Uno cards."

Abel faced me with hands on hips and a knowing smile.

I'd been Young Sherlocked.

I sighed. "I'm guessing you also know what he's using to blackmail me."

"I think I've figured it out," he said. Then he danced a *hasapiko* brush kick.

I clapped my hand to my forehead. "Did Brooke tell you?"

Abel shook his head. "The kid dancing in the

video wears the same watch as you and is about the same height. Plus, when I asked Brooke if it was you, she screamed 'I like pizza!' and ran away." At the confused look from me, he added, "We promised to never lie to each other."

I wanted to bury my head in my hands, but I knew Ryan was still roaming the student lounge. I couldn't give him the satisfaction of seeing me suffer.

Instead, I fixed my gaze on Abel. "You're right. About all of it. I'm on the video, and I'm being blackmailed."

Abel nodded sagely. "It's the ones you least expect who always turn out to be the master-minds."

I straightened up. "Well, I've finally had it! I won't do any more favors for him."

"Excellent!" Abel high-fived me. "What's the plan?"

I clenched my fist with steely resolve. "Oh,

it's gonna be good. It's gonna put Ryan in his place and show him that *nobody* messes with Tim Antonides!"

Abel cleared his throat. "You don't have a plan, do you?"

I relaxed my hand. "I was thinking about buying a soft pretzel," I said. "You want one?"

He shook his head and sat beside me. "You need to focus. I like what you said about putting Ryan in his place. I can help you with that."

My eyebrows lifted. "Help me?"

Abel shrugged. "Sure! What are friends for?"

"Friends?"

He studied me. "What's going on with you? You turning into a parrot?"

"Sorry." I felt my cheeks warm. "I'm just . . . not really used to having guy friends. But I'm through working for Ryan! What's the plan?"

"Keep working for him," said Abel.

I held up a finger. "Is there a Plan B?"

"Listen, right now Ryan has leverage over you." He leaned closer. "You need to get leverage over Ryan."

"What do you mean?" I asked.

"I mean, you need to find a reason for him to *not* rat on you," Abel explained. "Say . . . something that might embarrass him if it ever got out?"

A slow grin spread over my face. "You mean beat him at his own game. I like it!" I started writing in my notebook. "I could swing by his house this weekend. There's got to be something good there."

Abel nodded. "Maybe check his bedroom."

I shook my head. "There's nothing incriminating there. It's really clean." Abel raised an eyebrow, and I blushed. "I cleaned it."

He whistled through his teeth. "We have got to get you out of this. Forget his bedroom, then, and start looking elsewhere. Maybe his parents have some embarrassing baby photos?"

"He lives with his aunt," I said, pausing. "And he's also pretty good at figuring out what I'm up to. If I go wandering around his house, he's going to notice."

Abel and I were both quiet for a moment. Then he snapped his fingers and grinned.

"What if you're in front of him the whole time and someone else does the searching?"

I widened my eyes. "*You're* going to do it?"

"No, no. I'm thinking of someone else who's just as fast." He glanced past me to where Brooke and Vanessa were sitting.

"You want me to send Brooke in?" I asked.

"And Vanessa. She could be there to do some last-minute fixes to Ryan's look, and since you're trying to turn him into this great guy, what better way to test his limits than bringing in Brooke, the person he most despises?" Abel beamed at his own idea.

I rubbed my chin. "While V keeps him busy, Brooke could wander off to use the bathroom and 'accidentally' stumble across something embarrassing."

"But that means you have to let her in on the secret too," Abel pointed out.

I gave him a dubious look. "She *hates* Ryan. When she finds out what he's been up to, she'll kill . . ." I nodded and clapped my hands. "Okay, this plan works!"

He got to his feet, picking up his bag. "Talk to Brooke during your lunch. She'll help you set up a plan, and then she'll meet up with me. For now, act like we just finished the interview." He extended his hand, and I shook it.

"Thanks for all the help," I said, holding up my notebook for emphasis.

Abel gave a brief wave and walked off without another word.

I started for the lounge exit, but before I

could reach it, Ryan swooped over, throwing an arm around me. A small group of girls was watching and smiling, but for once they weren't smiling at me.

"Tim! Why don't you join us on the couch?" He glanced at the group of girls and flashed a grin. Then out of the corner of his mouth, he added, "I have no idea how to talk to them."

It was all I could do not to laugh and shout, "Serves you right!" After all, I was supposed to still be the humble servant.

"Actually, I have to go to the newsroom and do some work. People have been asking us for gift advice."

Ryan frowned. "When did we start giving gift advice?"

How was this idiot running my life?

"No, 'us' as in the advice column." I pointed to Brooke and V.

"Fine. Just give me something to talk about

with them." He nodded to the girls.

"Ask them about themselves, remember?" I said. "It makes you seem like a good listener."

He nodded, and I could see his mouth working as he repeated my instructions. "Thanks. I'll talk to you later," he said.

"Can't wait," I replied.

I headed up the hall, pausing at Locker 411 to see what new gift requests we'd gotten. I was starting to like them more than advice requests. My brain was already so full having to deal with Ryan, and coming up with gift ideas was way easier than dishing out advice. Why?

Because I had a system that I hadn't told Brooke, Heather, or Vanessa about.

Over the weekend I'd bought a magazine for girls, a magazine for boys, a magazine for women, and a magazine for men. I didn't read them; I just looked at the ads. That way, I had a huge bank of ideas at the ready. It was brilliant, it was simple, and if Brooke ever got mad, I could simply buy her a bottle of Teen Dream perfume ... or rip out the perfume strip from the magazines. Probably that.

I went inside and sat at my usual desk while across the room, Felix and Mary Patrick argued about the front page.

"Everyone's talking about the viral video issue," he said. "I have to follow it with something just as big. Don't you want more attention?"

"Of course I do!" said Mary Patrick. "I just don't think a piece on teen celebrities is the way to go. We're not some gossip magazine."

I shook my head and answered a gift request for someone's mom, flipping open a magazine. With my eyes closed, I waved my finger around and pressed it on one of the pages.

"Oh good. You're putting thought into these gifts," Heather's voice sounded beside me.

I opened my eyes and glanced at the page. My

finger had landed on a pair of diamond earrings.

"Come on, you have to admit that's a good gift." I grinned up at her.

She wrinkled her forehead. "You're not . . . answering all the gift requests like this, are you?"

I shook my head. "Not all. Just the ones that *I've* done."

Heather squinted at me. "Very funny. These kids genuinely want our help, you know."

"Which is why I'm randomly picking stuff in each price range," I said. "If you're looking for Brooke and V, by the way, they're in the student lounge."

"I know," she said. "But I saw Ryan Durstwich in there and . . . Man, he's even more obnoxious when he's cute."

I laughed. "You think?"

She nodded. "Don't get me wrong, he looks good and I'm glad he's got some decent manners now, but he really thinks he's all that." Her eyes widened, and she put a hand over her mouth. "Sorry, that was really mean. I know you're friends."

I snorted. "Me and Ryan? We're not friends."

"Really?" She tilted her head to one side. "But you spend so much time together."

First Abel noticed, now her? Was it really that obvious?

"We're working on a project. That's all," I said.

Heather smiled. "Well, thank goodness. Maybe you can try to set him straight," she said.

"Actually, I prefer to stay as far from him as possible," I said. "Can't have him picking up all my moves."

Heather laughed. "I know we tease you a lot, but you would be a great role model for him."

I stiffened but gave her a tight smile. "Nah," I said. "I don't really think that's a good idea."

"He needs someone like you around."

I shook my head and forced a laugh. "I don't . . ."

"Tim"—Heather put a hand on my arm—"don't be so modest. You can be a positive influence on Ryan, and it's good that he—"

"Ryan's blackmailing me with that dancing video," I said.

She might as well know. She was bound to find out from Vanessa or, pretty soon, Brooke.

Heather's grip tightened on my arm. "What?"

I shifted closer to her. "Look, don't say anything to anyone, okay? I'm handling it."

The concern didn't leave her eyes. "How has he been blackmailing you? Did you tell Mrs. H? The principal? Your parents?"

I held up a hand to stop her. "He's just been having me do a couple little tasks for him, nothing big"—I grabbed her arm as she started to move past me—"so just relax."

"He's been making you his servant?" Her

voice was barely above a whisper. "That's terrible! Why didn't you tell us earlier?"

"Because this is my problem to deal with, not yours," I said. "Like I said, I'm handling it. Or at least . . . I will be this weekend."

"What's happening this weekend?" she asked.

I explained Abel's idea, and she frowned. "That doesn't seem like the right way to deal with this. You should really let some adults know."

I shook my head. "All they'll do is scold Ryan. I need a way to stop him once and for all."

At the determined look on my face, Heather nodded. "Okay. How can I help?"

I gave her a grateful smile. "Right now, I think I'm good. If we get too many people involved, then Ryan's going to know I'm up to something."

Heather squeezed my arm. "If you do need anything, even just someone to talk to, you know I'm here."

The first bell rang, and we headed to our

lockers. I joined the students rushing to class and dropped into my homeroom desk just as the bell rang. The teacher did a quick head count and then settled into her chair with a magazine.

"Get started on any last-minute homework," she told us, and the room fell quiet.

I was about to reach for one of Ryan's assignments when I thought better of it and propped my binder up on my desk. Pulling my phone out of my pocket, I ducked behind the binder and texted Brooke.

I need your help with something this weekend.

There was no response for a minute or so and then, Sure. What's up?

Can you keep a secret? I texted back.

I haven't told anyone you're a spirited dancer yet, have I? she responded.

"Fair point," I muttered to myself, then texted, Ryan released the dance video, and he's blackmailing me into doing favors for him.

Two sets of classroom walls couldn't contain Brooke's voice.

"What?!" was her muffled cry.

Everyone in my homeroom looked up and glanced in the direction of the sound. The homeroom teacher frowned but went back to reading her magazine.

Congratulations, I texted Brooke. Yours is the voice heard round the world.

I will rip that kid to pieces! I will punch him through to the other side of the Earth!

Instantly, I was typing. No! You will do NOTHING to let him know you're on to him. Abel and I already have a plan to get me out of this mess.

You told Abel before you told me??? she texted back.

He figured it out on his own.

Brooke's response was hearts and smiley faces, along with the words I have the smartest boyfriend in the world!

I rolled my eyes and typed, We'll talk more at lunch.

But first we had to talk more about how great Ryan looked. At least . . . Vanessa did. When the four of us sat down to eat, she was grinning and gushing about all the compliments she'd gotten for Ryan's makeover.

"People say it's a huge improvement," she informed us.

"Sure." Brooke twisted spaghetti around her fork. "Fifty-five percent more evil."

"And that he really seems different."

"Different isn't always better," admonished Heather, opening her milk.

Vanessa hesitated for a moment but kept going. "And that he looks so cute."

"So do baby snakes," I said, taking a bite of my apple.

She sighed. "Awww, come on, guys. I know he was blackmailing Tim before, but he's changed!

He promised when I was doing his makeover."

I reached into my pocket and tossed the new task list on her tray. "You're right. He's changed. His handwriting's a little better."

Vanessa opened the paper and read it over with a frown. "That lying . . ." She slammed it down on the table. "But he pinkie swore!"

"And we all know how binding those can be." Brooke patted Vanessa on the back. "But luckily, Tim's finally going to take care of this." She looked at me. "What do you and Abel have planned?"

"I need to get some dirt on Ryan," I said. "Something juicy enough that he'll be too scared of people finding out to want to expose me anymore. I need you and Vanessa to help." I glanced at V, who nodded.

Brooke scooted closer. "How?"

"Ryan can't know I'm up to something, so Vanessa will do more makeover work with him, and you'll be there to help with his social skills. Then you'll conveniently disappear for a bit."

Brooke's eyes shone with excitement. "You want me to search for evidence."

"And I get to help with the distraction!" Vanessa clapped. "This is gonna be fun!"

"What's Heather gonna do?" asked Brooke.

"Nothing," Heather said with a sigh.

"It'll look suspicious if you're all there," I said, patting her arm.

V shook her head. "Not if Ryan doesn't see her. Brooke's going to need a lookout, right?"

"I could warn her if Ryan heads her way!" agreed Heather, straightening up.

"Already thought of that." I tapped my skull. "We're going to use the code phrase 'How about those Cubs?'"

"Yeah, because that won't seem suspicious after the first time," scoffed Brooke. "Plus, the Cubs are terrible this year."

She had a point.

I glanced at Heather. "You really want to help out?"

She nodded. "You're always there for me. I want to be there for you."

I rubbed my head and sighed. "Fine. But only Brooke goes searching, and *none* of you get noticed."

Heather and V high-fived, and Brooke placed a notepad in front of me.

"First things first, we need to case the joint." She tapped the page. "Draw me a map of the rooms on each floor so I can get around quicker."

"Uh . . . I don't know all of them," I said, "but I'll do the best I can." I started putting together a crude drawing.

Brooke nodded. "Now, when are you planning to be there tomorrow?"

I thought for a moment. "Maybe one?"

She punched something into her phone.

"Done. We'll take Ryan someplace in his house where there isn't bound to be anything to blackmail him with. Say . . . the kitchen."

I nodded. "Sure."

She looked up at Heather. "You'll be watching through the windows." She paused and looked at me. "I'm assuming there's at least one window in the kitchen?"

"Yep." I made sure to mark it on my drawing.

Brooke continued. "When I leave to start searching, if Heather sees Ryan make a move toward a door, she'll text me."

I passed the sketch to Brooke. "Here you go. I hope you can find something."

"Please," said Brooke. "I'm a detective in training." She narrowed her eyes and squared her jaw. "I'll find more dirt on Ryan than there are lice in his hair."

"Oh, Ryan doesn't have lice," said Vanessa. "I checked before I gave him a haircut."

Brooke made an exasperated sound. "V! I was having a dramatic moment."

"Sorry!"

I rolled my eyes at both of them. "See if you can come up with more than one secret," I told Brooke. "I'd like to have options."

"Oh, I'll steal his secrets." She nodded and narrowed her eyes again. "And then . . . we'll end this."

CHAPTER

9

Soccer Ninja

It wasn't the new and improved Ryan who answered his front door the next morning. It was the crumb-covered, greasy-haired original, complete with scowl. But as soon as he saw that Vanessa was with me, he brushed off his shirt and did his best to spike his hair.

It wasn't enough.

"*What* did you do to all my hard work?" cried Vanessa.

"I—I . . . My aunt doesn't like the new me," he stammered, backing away. At the look on V's face, I would've been terrified too. "She saw the clothes and the hair and figured I was up to something."

"Well, you are," I said, entering the house. "You're trying to convince people you aren't some slimy jerk."

"It looks like I got here just in time," Vanessa added, following me in with a tote bag slung over one shoulder. She pulled out an empty spray bottle and held it up. "Do you have a bathroom where I can fill this?"

Ryan pointed down the hall, and as soon as V walked away, he whirled around to face me.

"What is she doing here?" he asked in a harsh whisper.

"This is a dress rehearsal for Berkeley's get-together," I said. "You said you weren't sure what to wear."

The anger in Ryan's eyes dissolved. "Oh.

Well, you could've at least warned me!"

"I could have, but I thought it'd be more fun this way," I said.

Ryan shot me a look and moved to close the front door just as Brooke hurried onto the porch.

"Hold up!" she called.

"What—?" Ryan looked at me, and I grinned.

"Definitely more fun."

"Hey, mouth breather," Brooke greeted him, pushing her way into the house.

Ryan ignored her and continued to glare at me. "Why is *she* here?"

"I figured if you can talk to Brooke without any lamps or bones breaking, you can talk to anyone."

"Believe me, I'm not looking forward to this either," grumbled Brooke.

Earlier that morning she'd texted me, It's Heist Day! Yaaay!

Vanessa reappeared with a full spray bottle

and frowned at Ryan. "You're still wearing that?"

"No," he grumbled. "I'll change into my good outfit."

"If I were you, I'd be more upset that I only have one good outfit," I called after him as he headed upstairs.

"Ryan, do you need help?" added Vanessa.

"No! Just stay right there!" he shouted back.

As soon as I heard him walking above us, I said, "Okay, while he's gone we should—"

I turned toward my friends, but they were already in motion.

Brooke had opened one of the entertainment center doors and was skimming the DVDs and video game titles. Vanessa was inspecting the bookshelves.

"Nothing embarrassing here," whispered Brooke, closing the entertainment center.

"Dead zone," added V. "So are the downstairs bathroom and dining room."

"How do you know that?" I asked.

She brandished her squirt bottle and smiled. "I got lost on my way back."

"Smart!" I said.

"Shh. I think he's coming," whispered Brooke, jerking her head toward the staircase.

We all did our best to act casual as Ryan reappeared.

"Okay, let's do this," he said, tucking in his shirt. He started to take a seat on the couch, but I cleared my throat.

"Don't you think you should offer your guests something to drink?" I asked, gesturing to Vanessa and Brooke.

"Oh. Right," said Ryan. He turned to the girls. "Vanessa, would you like some soda? Brooke, a glass of poison?"

"Whoa, whoa, whoa." I wagged a finger. "Would you say that to anyone at Berkeley's party?"

Ryan sighed and spoke through clenched teeth. "Brooke, would you like some soda too?"

She rubbed her chin thoughtfully. "What kind?"

"The kind with bubbles in it," he said.

I cleared my throat again, and Ryan took a deep breath.

"We have root beer, cola, and diet cola."

"Do you have any juice?" asked Brooke.

Ryan forced a smile. "Yes. Would you like some juice?"

"What kind?" she asked.

He turned to me with an exasperated look. "Nobody at Berkeley's party is going to be this much of a pain."

"Just answer her question," I said.

Ryan groaned and turned back to Brooke. "We have apple juice and orange juice."

She nodded in satisfaction. "I'll take some orange juice, please."

"And I'll take some root beer," said Vanessa.

"Be right back," said Ryan, heading toward the kitchen.

We all followed right behind, and he glanced over his shoulder in confusion.

"You don't have to come with me," he said.

"I want to watch you walk," said Vanessa. "No look is complete without a good walk."

"I want to watch you pour my drink," said Brooke. "In case you really do put poison in it."

Ryan raised an eyebrow at me. "And what's your excuse?"

"I want to watch you interact with other people."

He muttered to himself and reached for the refrigerator door. Which happened to be by the kitchen window where Heather's head appeared.

"No!" Brooke cried, almost making Ryan drop a bottle of juice.

Heather quickly disappeared from sight.

"'No' what?" asked Ryan, his scowl returning.

"I changed my mind about the orange juice," she said. "Could I get apple juice instead?"

Ryan's lips pressed together, but he nodded and reached back into the refrigerator.

The top of Heather's ski cap appeared in the window as she tried to sneak another peek. I tapped my fingers on the glass.

Ryan popped his head out. "What was that?"

"Huh?" I glanced all around.

"What was what?" asked Brooke.

He closed the refrigerator door and glanced at the window. "I thought I heard something tap against the glass."

"It was a goose," said V.

I wanted to smack my hand to my forehead.

"A goose?" Ryan pushed past us to look out the window. If he happened to glance down, he'd spot one weird-looking bird.

"Up there!" I lifted his chin. "It took off already."

Ryan shrugged. "Must've lost its flock."

He turned back to the cupboard to grab some glasses and started pouring us each a drink.

As soon as the juice was in Brooke's glass, she grabbed it and downed it in one long continuous gulp, pushing the empty glass back to Ryan.

"Can I have another?" she asked.

"What are you, a camel?" Ryan shot back. This time, Vanessa nudged him. "I mean . . . sure."

He poured her another glass, and she chugged that one too.

"Gotta pee!" she announced when she set the glass down.

"I wonder why," said Ryan.

"Be right back!" she said, hurrying out of the kitchen. Ryan watched her head in the direction of the hallway bathroom. What he didn't see was her racing toward the stairs a minute later.

"How about offering Vanessa something to eat and a place to sit?" I suggested.

Ryan grabbed a jar of cookies and led the way to the living room. On our way out, I tapped the kitchen window again, and instantly, Heather reappeared. From where she stood, she could see into the living room, but unless Ryan had a reason to glance back in, he wouldn't notice her.

"Could we get to what's important?" asked V. "Ryan, you walk like you're carrying a sack of potatoes." She imitated his lumbering movements. "Let's work on your stride." She walked to the opposite end of the room, far from the hallway entrance. Even better. "Keep your eyes on me, shoulders back."

Vanessa had Ryan strut in front of her while she adjusted his spine, his shoulders, and even the way he swung his arms.

After a couple minutes, in which he definitely looked better, Ryan stopped and frowned.

"Brooke's been gone for a while."

"She did drink two glasses of juice," I pointed out.

"These are really good cookies," Vanessa added, holding one up. "What's the recipe?"

Ryan shook his head and walked toward the hallway bathroom. Where Brooke definitely wouldn't be.

"Do something," I whispered to Vanessa.

She nodded and called to Ryan, "Shoulders back!"

I stared at her. "That's not what I meant."

"Well, I'm sorry, but I can't ignore form that bad!" V told me.

From where we stood, I could hear Ryan open the bathroom door and mutter to himself. Then he passed the living room entrance, and I heard his feet hit the stairs.

I exchanged a panicked look with Vanessa.

"Brooke!" we both whispered.

Vanessa raced after Ryan, and I raced to the kitchen window, where Heather was already frantically texting. Then she produced a bike horn and honked it twice.

Not part of the original plan.

I couldn't stop to yell at her, though. Taking the steps two at a time, I found Vanessa waiting outside the door to Ryan's room while Ryan stood by his desk, frowning.

"Was that a bike horn?" he asked me.

I shook my head. "I farted. What are you doing in here?"

With a disgusted look, Ryan pointed to his computer. "I thought Brooke might be in here, messing with my stuff, but—"

There was the sound of a door opening down the hall and a toilet flushing as Brooke walked over to us. "What's going on?"

"What are you doing up here?" Ryan demanded.

"There wasn't any toilet paper in the downstairs bathroom, so I thought I'd use this one," she said. "Is that your bedroom?" She craned her neck to see, and that was when I spotted a massive cobweb in her hair.

Luckily, Ryan was too busy barring his doorway to notice.

"Of course it is, silly!" I reached up and tousled Brooke's hair while pulling at the cobweb.

"Dude!" Brooke gave me an annoyed look and smoothed it back down.

"So did you get the . . . uh . . . toilet paper you were looking for?" I asked.

"Yep!" She beamed a little too proudly for someone who'd simply gone to the bathroom.

"Good," said Vanessa. "And while we're here, Ryan, I want to see your best shirts."

He nodded and took a couple steps into his room. "Wait right there. All of you," he said, not taking his eyes off Brooke as he sidled over to his closet.

My phone vibrated with a new text message.

"While you guys do that, Brooke, ask Ryan a little about himself," I said, taking my phone out of my pocket. The message was from Heather.

Everything okay?

Yes, I responded while Brooke asked, "So, Ryan, I noticed there aren't any family pictures on the walls. What's up with your parents?"

Ryan stopped midreach for a shirt and frowned. "That's none of your business."

"Ooh, touchy subject. Gotcha," she said. Then after a second: "Are they alive or dead?"

"Brooke!" said V.

"No, it's fine," said Ryan, sitting on his desk chair. "My parents were killed one night while leaving an opera. They walked down some dark alley, and a guy was waiting for them. My parents offered to give him all their money, but he wanted their lives."

Brooke pressed a hand to her chest. "That's horrible!"

I snorted. "It's also the plot of Batman."

Brooke narrowed her eyes. "Hey."

Ryan smiled. "Yeah, it is. The truth is . . ." He shrugged. "I don't know what happened to them. My aunt Sue's been caring for me for as long as I can remember." He made a face. "Well, not caring. More like . . . making sure I don't die."

For a brief moment Ryan almost seemed like a decent person. But then he followed it up with "She's more like my maid, I guess."

I rolled my eyes, and Brooke said, "*There's* the real Ryan."

"What's that supposed to mean?" he asked with a frown.

"Nothing." She checked her watch. "This has

been a great chat, but I should probably leave. V, you coming?"

Vanessa looked up from the shirts she was sorting through. "Huh? Yeah, just give me a second."

"I should probably go too," I said. "Dance practice."

I'd actually already missed dance practice, but I didn't want to hang out at Ryan's house without my friends there.

Brooke started down the stairs, and I nudged Vanessa's arm. "Let's go, V."

She nodded and handed two shirts to Ryan. "Wear this one if you can get the stain out." She wiggled the hanger. "Or this one if you can find the button and get your aunt to sew it back on."

Ryan took them from her. "I'll have someone take care of it," he said, eyes darting to me.

Oh, I definitely didn't feel sorry for this kid.

"Well, gotta go!" I said by way of answer. I grabbed V's arm and tugged her toward the stairs.

Ryan walked us to his front door, and my friends and I strolled down the street without another word. The second we rounded the corner, though, I turned to Brooke.

"Did you really find something?"

"Of course!" She held up her phone.

"We want to see too!" Heather said, running over with Abel.

"What's up?" I grinned and gave him a fist bump.

"Had to see how my plan played out," he said.

"There were a few hiccups," I said. "And a horn . . ." I looked to Heather, who pointed at Brooke.

"Her idea! In case she didn't feel her phone vibrate from my text," said Heather.

Brooke waved a dismissive hand. "None of

that matters. Check out all these juicy pictures I found!"

The five of us crowded around.

The first image was of Toddler Ryan sitting *in* the toilet.

"Eww!" squealed Heather. All of us giggled.

The next image was again of Toddler Ryan, but this time he was wearing lipstick and chewing on it at the same time. After that was one of him about to kiss a girl who was screaming and trying to escape.

Brooke flipped through several more photos of Ryan through the years in different ridiculous situations, even a picture where he was clearly trying to be cool while wearing a fake mustache and leather jacket.

"Where did you get all these?" I asked between fits of laughter.

"They were in his aunt's bedroom," she said. "She had a whole box of photos labeled 'Precious

Memories.' So I was thinking," said Brooke, "that we take these precious memories and make a slideshow with silly music of our own. We can send it to Ryan and let him know two can play his game." She smiled triumphantly.

"Mission accomplished!" said Abel, high-fiving her.

"Man, I hope he calls our bluff," said Brooke, zooming in on one of the photos. "I'd love to embarrass him."

"Yeah," I said with a smile.

But for some reason, I didn't really share her enthusiasm.

Later that afternoon I lay on my bed, staring at my phone. Brooke had texted me the pictures of Ryan, but I hadn't done anything with them, even though I knew exactly which song I'd set them to ("Bibbidy Bobbidi Boo").

I could hear noise from downstairs as Gabby came back from folk dance practice, and a minute later, she was thundering up to the second floor.

"You're here!" she said, bouncing onto the bed beside me. "Everybody missed you at practice."

"Really? How was it?" I asked.

"Oh, it was great," she said. "My invisible dance partner has the best form." She gave me a pointed look, and I winced.

"Sorry," I said. "I had to take care of something important. Is Uncle Theo mad?"

"That you've missed almost every practice the last couple weeks?" She smirked. "What do you think?"

I sat up. "I should talk to him."

Gabby shook her head. "He already took off. Something about a meeting with the show choreographer. How was . . . whatever you were up to?"

"Good," I said, nodding over and over.

"Then what's with the frown?" She poked the corner of my mouth with her finger, and I squirmed away.

"Things just aren't turning out like I'd hoped," I said.

"Gee, can you make that any vaguer?" she asked.

I sighed. "Ryan's the one who took the video of me and shared it with the school." I paused for an explosive reaction, but all Gabby did was nod.

"Yeah, I already pieced that together myself."

"And you're not going on a murderous rampage?" I marveled.

"Nah. He was nice enough to blur your face out of the video," she said.

"Because he's blackmailing me with the unblurred version."

Gabby sat up straight, eyes narrowing. "*That* I did not know. What's this jerk's address?"

I smirked. "Two days ago you were gushing about how cute he was."

"He can be both," she informed me, hopping

off the bed. "Now how are we going to take this cute jerk down?"

I flopped back onto the bed and stared at the ceiling. "Don't bother. I already have what I need to get revenge."

"And you seem thrilled about it," she noted with a wry smile. "So what's the problem?"

"Now that I have a chance," I said, shaking my head, "I can't go through with it."

Gabby pursed her lips and nodded. "Because it's not you. You might be a liar and a loud eater and a huge flirt and . . . a great brother," she finished after a glare from me. "But you're not out to hurt anyone, even if they deserve it."

"But if I don't beat Ryan at his own game, he'll always win." I punched a pillow with my fist.

"Not if you don't play his game," she said, sitting back down.

I propped myself on an elbow. "It's not that easy. I can't quit this, just like I can't quit folk dancing. The consequences are too disastrous. I'm trying to make friends with the guys, and if they find out the truth . . ."

"Well, you can't keep letting Ryan blackmail you."

"I know."

"Then you have to have your revenge," Gabby reasoned.

"But I can't!" I said.

Gabby gave an exasperated sigh. "Tim, it's a mess all around, but unless you have a third option, you either have to get out or get even."

It wasn't the advice I wanted to hear, but I didn't have much of a choice. I spent Sunday weighing my options and trying to think of other ones, but they all required bribing Ryan in some way.

On Monday morning my friends pounced as soon as I walked into the student lounge.

"I'm so excited!" Brooke gushed. "Please,

please, please let me be there when you tell Ryan."

"Or did you already do it?" asked Vanessa.

Heather studied my face. "If Tim did, I'm guessing it didn't go well."

"No." I rubbed the back of my neck. "Guys, I appreciate all the hard work you put into this, but . . . I can't go through with it." I turned to Abel, who was standing next to Brooke. "Sorry. It was a good idea."

"It's cool," he said.

The girls were not as okay with it.

"What?!" all three of them cried.

"He tried to destroy you!" said Brooke.

I shook my head. "It doesn't matter. I can't stoop to his level."

"Well, *I* can," Brooke said with a deep scowl. "If you won't blackmail Ryan into silence, then I will."

I glanced at Abel, who reached over and

snatched Brooke's phone away.

"Abel! Give it!" She jumped up and down, trying to wrest it from him while he went through each image and deleted it. When he was done, he handed Brooke her phone.

"Sorry, but that was for your own good," he said. "'If once you start down the dark path—'"

"Don't quote *Star Wars* at me," she said with a pout, searching through her photos.

"It's *The Empire Strikes Back*, actually," he said. "And I permanently deleted those pics so there's no point in looking."

Instead of raging at him, Brooke shook her phone at me. "Dang it, Tim! We had him!"

Heather grabbed her arm. "No, Tim's right. Revenge was a bad idea. It's better to take the high road."

I gave her a grateful smile and tried to remember her words when Ryan caught up with me later and handed me both of the shirts that

Vanessa had handed *him* on Saturday.

"I think you know what to do," he said with a wink.

I sighed and twirled the shirts on their hangers. If I knew what to do, I sure wouldn't be holding his laundry.

That afternoon, when Uncle Theo picked me and Gabby up for practice, he greeted us with a soft smile and a mild, "Hello, you two. How was school?"

Gabby and I exchanged a look. Was my sadness spreading?

"Uh . . . fine," I said. "Are you okay, Uncle Theo?"

"Or are you mad at Tim for missing practices?" added Gabby.

I elbowed her.

"What, like nobody was thinking that?" she asked.

"Actually," said Uncle Theo, "this does concern

Tim missing practices."

"I know I'm behind," I said, "but when we get to the studio, I'll pick up right where we left off."

Uncle Theo sighed. "You won't be going to the studio, Timotheos. I'm dropping you off at home."

"What?" I leaned forward in my seat. "Why?"

He was quiet for a moment, but I could see his lips moving, as if he was trying to find the right way to answer.

"The choreographer is kicking you out of the holiday show."

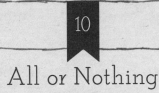

CHAPTER
10
All or Nothing

"**W**hat?" cried Gabby.

"You're kidding, right?" I asked with a nervous grin. "This is a joke."

Uncle Theo shook his head. "Mr. Humphries never jokes when it comes to dance."

"So I don't get to perform at the museum?" I could hear my voice coming out as a whine, but couldn't stop it. "Why not?"

"He said you're not up to grade-A performance standards, and . . . I have to agree with him." Uncle Theo gave me a pained look. "Right now, you're barely a C level."

"But . . . I'm really good! People at the dance studio told me!" I pointed at him. "You've told me!"

Uncle Theo pulled into traffic. "You *are* a great dancer, Timotheos. But you don't know all the moves, and you missed practices. Mr. Humphries wants to give the Museum of Science and Industry our very best."

"I can do that!" I jabbed myself in the chest. "I know I had a bunch of stuff going on that got in the way, but I'm committed now. Please let me do this!"

"Unfortunately, it's not up to me." Uncle Theo glanced at me in the rearview mirror, his expression close to disbelief. "And I had no idea this meant so much to you."

I fell back against my seat, silent.

To be honest, I hadn't known it meant so much either. But now that it was being taken from me, I realized that I wanted to dance the *sirtaki* and the *hasapiko* and the *kalamatiano*. I wanted to kick and twirl and have everyone watch and clap along. I wanted to be a Greek folk dancer.

I stretched forward with renewed purpose and grabbed Uncle Theo's shoulder. "Please, let me talk to Mr. Humphries and try to convince him. If I practice really hard, like, every free hour, I can make this work. I was wrong to goof off so much, but I really do want this."

"I can train him at home, too!" piped up Gabby.

We reached the intersection where the dance building and our neighborhood went in opposite directions. Uncle Theo pulled to the side of the road and twisted in his seat to look back at me.

"It's less than a week until the performance. You will have to work very hard. I can plead your case, but you can't let me down."

I nodded emphatically. "I promise."

Uncle Theo regarded me solemnly and then

faced forward, put the car into gear, and drove toward the studio. I breathed a sigh of relief and leaned against the window.

Once we reached the studio, Uncle Theo filled the other dancers in on what was happening. They seemed as shocked as I was and agreed to train me as fast as they could. Their overwhelming support might have actually choked me up if one of the men hadn't immediately pointed to the dance floor and demanded a *hasapiko*.

"Uh . . . sure," I said, very aware that all eyes were on me. "Could I get some music, though?"

Someone turned on the stereo, and I held my arms out by my sides, slowly doing a step-hop onto my left foot before raising my right leg and stepping back with it. Then I raised my left leg before stepping back into a cross kick. The other dancers clapped while I moved, and Gabby put an arm across one of my shoulders, falling into step beside me. We smiled at each other as the tempo picked up and we started to dance faster. Soon, a woman had joined me on the other side and then a man stepped in next to her. By the end of the song, everyone was dancing and smiling, and this time when Uncle Theo smiled at me, I understood.

Our dancing wasn't just silly leg kicks and skirts. It was tradition and family and friends, celebrating our heritage together.

"Excuse me," Uncle Theo told the rest of the dancers. "I have to make a phone call." He winked at me and stepped out of the studio.

Before someone could tell me what to dance again, I asked, "Can we practice the *divaratikos*?"

I was so swept up in the movements that I didn't even see Uncle Theo return until we took a water break. Thankfully, he was smiling.

I rushed over to him, wiping sweat off my face. "Am I back in?"

Uncle Theo crossed his arms over his chest.

"I told Mr. Humphries we needed to show future generations that our way of life isn't just the old way; it is the way for all!"

"And?" asked Gabby, who had followed me over.

Uncle Theo leaned toward us. "If Tim can impress Mr. Humphries at Friday's rehearsal, he's in."

"Yes!" I jumped up and hugged Uncle Theo. "I won't let you down, I promise!"

Uncle Theo chuckled and patted my back. "Come, Timotheos. Let's see what you've learned."

We practiced for another half hour before a different group, who had booked the room, arrived. My family and I had to leave, but I wasn't ready to stop. As soon as we got back to the house, I started pushing furniture aside in the living room.

"Can you guys help me?" I asked Gabby and

Uncle Theo. "The couch is really heavy."

"Your parents aren't going to like this," said Uncle Theo. He squatted and picked up the couch all by himself.

"Sure they are," I said, swinging my arms and cracking my neck. "I'm embracing my roots!"

Gabby found some Greek music on her phone and cranked it up. We practiced our full routine, and even though there were a few places I stumbled and got mixed up, overall I had most of it down. While Gabby and I danced, Uncle Theo coached.

"Again," I said when the last note played.

Uncle Theo restarted the music.

The second time was a little better, but I stumbled a bit when my phone started to vibrate with text messages and calls from Ryan. Luckily, Uncle Theo knew right away what the distraction was and danced my phone into the other room.

"Tonight, there is only Greece!" he hollered. "*Opa!*"

"*Opa!*" Gabby and I shouted back.

Shortly after, the front door opened and Mom and Dad walked in with groceries. Like I thought, they weren't upset at all about the dust we were making. Mom was watching in amusement, and Dad dropped his bag and jumped in on my other side, grabbing my hand and side-stepping like he'd been doing it his whole life . . . which he probably had.

When the music stopped, I panted and shouted, "Again!"

Gabby shook her head and made a time-out gesture with her hands. "I need water! And food!"

"That's a good idea," Dad said, clapping a hand on Uncle Theo's back. "What say we fire up the grill?"

"But it's thirty degrees outside!" Mom said with a laugh.

"I've got to have some kabobs," Dad said over his shoulder. "I'm feeling inspired!"

Mom looked from me to Gabby. "So what brought on this sudden surge in dancing?"

"We're trying to make sure Tim gets in the performance."

Mom frowned. "Why wouldn't he?"

"It's a long story," I said, shaking my head.

"Okay." She kissed the top of my head. "You'll tell us when you're ready, I know." A grin spread over her face. "For now, do you want to see if we can make s'mores before Dad and Uncle Theo throw any meat on the grill?"

The next morning it felt like I'd dislocated a rib. My entire body ached as I rolled out of bed, but it was Tuesday, which meant I only had three days to perfect my performance.

With every step down the staircase I groaned and whined. "Can we please put a fireman's pole in this place?" I asked my parents, who were already in the kitchen.

"How can a kid who plays so many sports be so out of shape?" asked Dad.

"Dancing doesn't exactly work the same muscles as football," I said.

When Gabby hobbled downstairs, she looked almost as rough as I felt. "Tim, I'm going to kill you if you don't make it into the show," she said.

"You guys just need to stretch out," Mom said, rubbing one of Gabby's arms.

"We'll have plenty of time to do that today," I said, giving my sister an evil grin. "Because there's even more practicing to do!"

Gabby moaned and buried her head in Mom's shoulder. "Save me, Mommy."

"You know, technically, Gabby knows all the

dance moves, so she can just watch while you do them," said Dad.

"No," Gabby said with a forlorn sigh. "It works better with two people." She pointed at me. "You'd better be getting me a really great Christmas present!"

"Oh shoot!" I gulped down my orange juice. "I promised Brooke I'd help with gift requests before school."

Dad checked his watch. "If you can be ready to go in ten minutes, I can take you on my way to the dentist."

Despite my screaming muscles, I hurried back up the stairs and into my school clothes, pausing only for a second when I picked up my backpack. I'd never finished Ryan's homework.

"Tim, you ready?" Dad called from downstairs.

"Yep!" I scooped up my bag and followed him out to the car.

Fifteen minutes later I was staggering into the newsroom with a pained expression.

"Oh, come on. Helping out isn't that bad," said Vanessa.

"It's not that," I said, shifting the weight of my bag.

"Here, let me." Heather grabbed it while I rubbed one of my shoulders.

Brooke raised an eyebrow. "You know you don't have to carry the whole library with you."

I laughed and waved her off. "It's not books; it's lots and lots of dance practice. And I'm guessing you're not mad at me anymore?"

She shrugged and smiled. "At the end of the day it was your choice. But I gotta say it was a fun spy caper."

"Yeah, it kinda was." I smiled back. "So how's it going with the gift advice?" I asked, pulling a desk over to my friends. Nobody answered right away.

"It's . . . ," began Heather.

"Well . . . ," said V.

"Terrible." Brooke chewed her lip. "It's a lot harder to pick gifts for strangers than I thought. I keep making a list of five or six options because I'm afraid the first one won't be good enough. And they're *still* not right."

I nodded. "I've seen articles about what to get your favorite geek or bookworm, and it's never anything *I'd* want."

"Well, of course not," said Heather. "You're not just a bookworm. You're also an athlete and a museum lover and a theater buff."

"Are you guys doing any better at this?" I asked her and Vanessa.

"My go-to answer is a gift card," V said with a grin.

I chuckled. "Smart." I looked at the surveys and catalogs strewn across the desk, a valiant but failed attempt to define people by interests. "You know, I think our extra article for the newspaper is right here."

"Where?" Brooke asked glumly. "Under the survey where we got a score of negative one million?"

"All of this." I gestured to the table. "We can do a piece on how we tried giving advice on people, not problems, and how it didn't work."

Vanessa snorted. "Mary Patrick would love that."

Brooke's eyes lit up. "She *would* love that! We could even say this was an experiment!" She gripped my shoulders. "Tim, you're brilliant! I wish I'd thought of it."

I pointed at her. "I'll give you credit for the idea if you write the article."

"Deal!" Brooke's smile faded. "Uh-oh. Your BFF's here."

I glanced past her to see Ryan in the doorway.

He was back to his new-and-improved self, minus the smile. "Can I talk to you?" he asked me, not even bothering to acknowledge my friends.

"He looks pretty mad," whispered Heather. "Do you think he figured out what Brooke did?"

"I put it all back!" said Brooke.

"It's not about that. Give me a sec," I told my friends, pulling Ryan into the hall.

"You didn't return my calls or texts," he said with a huff.

"Good morning to you, too," I said. "I see you're back in Ryan 2.0 mode." I took in his clean clothes and styled hair. "And I was busy last night."

He clucked his tongue. "Well, you're just going to have to make up for it today. My house still needs to be vacuumed, and my aunt told me I need to do all the laundry."

"I can't," I said. "I've got dance practice."

Ryan shrugged. "It'll have to wait. Or do I need to remind you of what will happen?"

There it was again. That threat to ruin my life.

Which he was already doing every day.

I wasn't sure if it was because my body felt like it was on fire or because I'd done the right thing and Ryan still treated me badly, *or* if it was simply because I was *so* close to missing out on the museum performance. At that moment, I truly was done.

I took a step forward and stared Ryan down. A flicker of surprise crossed his face, but he held my gaze.

"I'm sorry your life is hard and your family isn't the greatest," I said. "And I'm sorry you think I'm spoiled and deserve to be tortured. And for the hundredth time, I'm sorry that I made fun of you in class and everyone laughed!" I shifted even closer to him. "But I will *never* let you control me again." I clenched my jaw. "So go ahead. Tell the world."

Ryan blinked and backed up a few paces. "They're all going to laugh at you."

"Great," I said. "I love to make people laugh."

I crossed my arms, heart pounding a mile a minute in my chest.

"Are you guys done yet?" Brooke poked her head out of the newsroom. "Did I miss the fight?"

For a moment Ryan continued to stand there. Then he smirked. "We're not done. Not by a long shot," he said, and sauntered away.

Vanessa and Heather crowded the doorway alongside Brooke. "What happened?" V asked as we watched Ryan storm down the hall.

"I'm pretty sure I committed social suicide," I said with a tight smile. "I just told Ryan he couldn't blackmail me anymore and that I was fine with everyone knowing my secret."

"Awesome!" Heather held up her hand so I could high-five it. "I mean, not the part about everyone knowing, but the part about you finally standing up to Ryan!"

I high-fived her back. "You should probably bask in the glory of my presence while I'm still popular."

"Awww." Brooke squeezed my arm. "I'll still be your friend, even when you become a ridiculous internet meme."

During homeroom I sat next to Gabby, and we did foot movements under our desk to practice our dances. Since we were trying to look completely innocent, it wasn't long before we were cracking ourselves up. At lunch, my sister joined me in the newsroom, despite Mary Patrick's protests, so we could practice some more.

"This is a newsroom, not a dance hall!" she cried as papers blew off her desk when we moved past.

"There's nowhere else to practice," I said.

"How about the gym or . . ." She frowned. "Can I help you?" she asked someone behind me.

I turned and saw a girl timidly waiting by the doorframe.

"Someone gave me a note to give to you," she told Mary Patrick, still standing by the door and holding out the paper.

"Do I look like my arms will stretch that far?" asked Mary Patrick. "Bring it to me!"

The girl jumped but hurried forward, waiting just long enough for Mary Patrick's fingers to touch the paper before releasing it and hurrying away.

"'Tim Antonides is the dorky teen from the dancing video,'" Mary Patrick read aloud. Then she crumpled the note and threw it into the garbage. "Seriously, the gym or the library," she told me. "Please, dance anywhere but here."

Gabby ignored her and reached into the trash

can. "Someone just spilled your secret!" she said, gawking at me.

"Yeah, Ryan," I said. "I finally told him no more."

My younger sister (by three minutes) hugged me. "I'm so proud of you!"

"And you can be rest assured, I am *not* printing that gossip in the paper." Mary Patrick huffed.

"Actually," I said, "I think you should put it in. But could you wait and add it at the last minute? I don't want anyone to leak the info before Monday."

Mary Patrick gave me a dubious look. "You're really okay with people knowing? I thought it was a big secret."

I shook my head. "It shouldn't have been. Please, print the piece." I glanced at Gabby. "And mention that my sister and I performed at the Museum of Science and Industry."

Mary Patrick picked up her notebook. "Fine. I'll put something together. In the library. So you two can dance." She held up a finger. "But this doesn't count as the advice column's extra holiday piece."

"Actually, we came up with a different idea for that," I said. "And it'll be on your desk by Friday."

Mary Patrick smiled. "It better be."

"You're pretty confident you're going to make it into the show, aren't you?" Gabby asked as Mary Patrick walked away.

"Actually, I'm still pretty terrified," I confessed. "But if I know it's going to be in print, it just means I'll practice even harder." I positioned myself next to her. "Ready to go again?"

For the next few days my life itself was a whirlwind dance. But when Friday afternoon came and the lyres started playing and my dance mates started the *sirtaki*, I was right there with them, step for step.

When practice was over, Mr. Humphries, the choreographer, looked me up and down and said, "Your blouse is missing a button. Have it fixed before the show tomorrow."

And it was all I could do not to throw in a twirl.

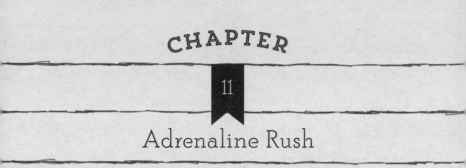

CHAPTER

11

Adrenaline Rush

"Let's go, let's go, let's go!" Mom's voice carried upstairs as she pounded a fist against the staircase wall. "We have to beat traffic, park, and hit the gift shop!"

"That last one isn't as high a priority!" Dad's voice followed hers.

I charged downstairs in my street clothes with my gym bag over one shoulder, but Mom pointed behind me.

"Nope. You need to be in costume when we get there," she said. "Unless you want to duck behind a Christmas tree and pull a Clark

Kent—into-Superman move."

"Please don't compare Tim to Superman," Gabby said from the top of the stairs.

"Hey, I've got the tights," I said, running past her into the bathroom to change.

She banged on the door. "I wasn't done in there!"

"I'll be right out!" I promised.

I slipped into my folk costume and dropped my street clothes in the bag just as Gabby started banging on the door again. "I need the hair spray."

The second I unlocked the door she pushed her way in and reached for an aerosol can and spritzed, creating a sticky, wet cloud of perfume.

"Couldn't you have waited until I got out?" I fanned the air and backed away, coughing.

"Tim, are you dressed?" Mom's voice called again.

"On my way!" I took the steps two at a time and slid down the banister at the end.

She looked me over and nodded approvingly. "Grab your jacket and get into the car. I'll wrestle the hair spray away from your sister."

"Be careful!" I called. "It's extra-strength hold!"

Dad was already waiting behind the steering wheel, checking his phone for traffic updates. "We're cutting it close," he informed me as I buckled myself into the back. "Where are Mom and Gabby?"

"We're here!" called Mom.

"Where's Uncle Theo?" asked Gabby.

"He's going to meet us at the museum," said Dad. "Something about picking up his girlfriend."

I widened my eyes. "They've gone from dating to being a couple?"

"Awww! Good for them," said Gabby.

"It's a Christmas miracle," I agreed.

"Be nice," Mom said, reaching behind her seat to squeeze my knee.

Dad put the car in gear, and soon, we were in Chicago traffic.

"There's no way I'm going to find close parking," he said. "I'll drop you off up front and meet you inside."

"Fine by me," I said. Even though I was more comfortable being a Greek folk dancer, I still wasn't comfortable enough to walk several city blocks in full costume.

Gabby, Mom, and I hurried into the museum and found Uncle Theo waiting by the ticket booth.

"Sorry!" Mom said before he could speak. "We were running a little behind."

"It's fine." Uncle Theo hugged Gabby and me and then steered us up the escalator to the main hall.

As soon as the rotunda was in sight, the spirit of Christmas was overwhelming. Beautiful trees with hundreds of ornaments and twinkling lights lined the entrance to the escalators and the edges of the rotunda. The trees had all been decorated by different community groups, so each was something special. At the center of the floor space was a massive forty-five-foot tree decorated with a superhero theme.

"Awesome," I said in a soft voice.

"Too cool," agreed Gabby.

Kids were darting around one side of a big tree, catching fake snowflakes, but there was no time for us to play if we wanted to make it to our performance. Uncle Theo led the way to a room labeled "Holiday Stage," which was already crowded.

"Are all these people here to see us?" Gabby asked, wide-eyed.

"Us and the other Greek performance troupes," said Uncle Theo. "It's an entire show-case. Ah. Here are our people!"

He pointed to the side of the stage, where Mr.

Humphries was wildly waving his arm overhead.

"It's about time," he said when we ran over. "We were going to have to open with the second act. Are you ready to go?"

Instantly, my heart hammered faster in my chest, but I nodded and shrugged off my jacket.

Mr. Humphries signaled the emcee onstage, who nodded and approached the microphone.

"Ladies and gentlemen, for our first performance showcasing Christmas in Greece, I present to you the Berryville Greek Society!" He clapped his hands and stepped away while the audience joined in on the applause.

Gabby gave me a nervous smile, and I squeezed her hand.

"Let's do this!" I whispered as we fell into line.

Our dance troupe took to the stage and got into position, facing the audience.

Suddenly, there was a chant of "Go, Tim, go!

Go, Gabby, go!" from the right side of the room.

My sister and I looked out at my friends, sitting in the crowd and waving. We grinned and nodded as the rest of the audience politely laughed.

Then the music began. We were transported halfway around the world. Arms wrapped across shoulders as we shuffled and stepped, and the audience clapped along in time to the music. When it grew faster, they increased their clapping and threw in some hoots. (I'm pretty sure that was Brooke.) Between the bright stage lights and all the dancing, it wasn't long before the entire troupe was sweating, but it was the best, most fun workout I'd ever had.

When our last number ended, the audience stood and applauded and hooted some more. The emcee ushered us offstage so the next troupe could go on, and my friends hurried to meet us.

"That was so cool!" V said, giving me a hug.

She stepped away, wiping her arms. "And a little sweaty."

"Sorry," I said with a laugh, and turned to Gil, who had his hand raised for a high-five.

"So jealous, man," he told me. "Makes me want to get my family onstage for some Polynesian dancing!"

"You were amazing," agreed Heather.

"Thanks!" I told her, leaning in for a hug.

When I turned to Brooke, she shrugged. "I must say, after all the fun I've made of you, it was actually a pretty awesome performance."

"Anybody who wants to tease you about *that* has to go through me," agreed Abel.

"Thanks, dude." I gave them each a brief hug, and the time on my watch caught my eye. "Shoot! It's already four o'clock!"

Brooke squinted at me. "Are your shoes about to turn into pumpkins or something?"

"No, Berkeley Dennis's party starts at five o'clock. I've got to get out of here!" I waved to my friends. "Sorry, guys! Thanks so much for coming!" I tugged on Uncle Theo's sleeve, and he turned around. "Sorry to run, but I've got something else to get to."

Uncle Theo nodded and then hugged me. "You were amazing, Timotheos. Thank you for giving it your all." He stepped back. "Before you leave, I want you to meet my girlfriend. Sue?"

A woman stepped away from where she'd been talking to my parents.

A woman I recognized.

Ryan's aunt.

She smiled when she saw me. "Hello, Tim!"

Uncle Theo glanced from her to me in confusion. "You know each other?"

"Her nephew goes to school with me," I said. I had to fight back a laugh.

Ryan, the kid who made fun of my dancing, might someday be part of an entire family of dancers.

"Well, it's nice to meet you as Uncle Theo's girlfriend," I told Sue, offering my hand.

"Likewise, for you being his nephew," she said with a chuckle.

"Sorry to bail," I said, "but . . ."

Uncle Theo shooed me away. "Go, go, go!"

I moved past them and grabbed Dad's arm. "It's Adrenaline time!"

Dad checked his watch. "Yikes! You're right." He turned to Mom. "Ready?"

"But I haven't been to the gift shop!" she said.

"I can give her and Gabby a ride if you need me to," said Uncle Theo.

"Best big brother ever," Mom said, kissing his cheek.

"Okay, okay." He brushed it off, blushing.

Dad kissed Mom and squeezed Gabby before putting an arm around me. "Let's go!"

The way Dad dodged and ducked through the crowd with me in tow, you'd have thought he was Adrenaline himself. We were out of the museum in record time and sprinting to the car.

Out of the city, however . . . That was a different story.

"How can there be more traffic going out than there is coming in?" he mumbled as we inched along.

I glanced in the backseat and moaned. "That's not the worst part. I forgot my street clothes!"

"What?" Dad looked over and almost rear-ended a minivan.

"Look out!" I said.

He slammed on the brakes. "How did you forget your clothes?"

"I must have left them in the bathroom when

Gabby was doing her hair!" I clapped my hand to my forehead. "I can't go to Adrenaline's party like this!"

"Well, at least you have your jacket," he mused with a hopeful smile. Then he looked me over and frowned. "Oh, no, you don't. Your mother is going to *kill* me."

I twisted around to check the backseat for any stray T-shirts or sweatpants . . . anything I might have left behind over the years in the car. All I found was some old french fries and pocket change.

"I need you to turn around and face front, buddy." Dad patted my leg.

I did as he said. "And I need you to trade clothes with me."

"Ha!" Dad shook his head. "I can't fit into your clothes, and I'm definitely not driving around town in my underwear. We'll just have to swing by the house first."

"There's no time!" I pointed to the digital display on the dash. "Who knows how long Adrenaline's going to be there?"

Dad sighed. "Then I'm sorry, buddy. You'll either have to miss meeting him or go dressed like that."

I glanced down at my clothes. Everybody was going to find out my secret on Monday when the paper came out, anyway. It was time for me to own who I was.

I took a deep breath and nodded. "To the party!"

Dad smiled and skirted around a car. "To the party!"

When we arrived at Berkeley's house, Dad and I both stared in awe for a moment. Berkeley lived in a mansion that looked like it belonged on a show for celebrity homes.

"You said this kid goes to school with you?" Dad asked. "Does he show up in a helicopter?"

I gazed up at the flags on the roof. "He probably has his butler carry him all the way." I pushed open the car door and glanced at Dad. "Could you wait here, in case I feel supremely humiliated and need to run out?"

Dad nodded. "Are you sure you don't want me to go in with you?"

I shook my head. "Thanks, but I've got to do this on my own."

I wasn't sure if it was my imagination, but the walk up to Berkeley's front door seemed to take forever. When I looked over my shoulder at Dad, the car seemed miles away. I could hear the voices of several people, along with one adult voice occasionally chuckling and joining in, coming from inside the manor. My finger shook when I reached for the doorbell, and I had to steady it with my other hand.

The chimes played *Für Elise*, and after what seemed like a minute later, the door clicked open.

Berkeley's eyebrows went up when he saw my outfit, and he smiled. "Wow, I feel underdressed. Come on in."

That was all.

He didn't laugh. Didn't point and call out to the others to come make fun of me.

I stood there, staring stupidly, waiting for a stronger reaction. "I'm a Greek—"

"Folk dancer." He finished for me, nodding. "I thought that was you in the video that was going around. You've got some skills!"

I stood there with my mouth open. "You knew? And you still wanted me to come over?"

Finally, Berkeley laughed. "Well, yeah, why wouldn't I? You're a dancer, not a serial killer." He opened the door wider so I could go in. "So did you have practice this morning or something?"

"Uh . . ." I waved down the walkway at Dad, who returned the wave and drove away. "My sister and uncle and I were part of a Christmas

Around the World show at the Museum of Science and Industry," I explained.

"Cool!" he said. "I love that place. My parents go to a big fund-raiser there every year. I'll bet it's fun to be part of the experience."

"It totally was," I agreed, feeling myself relax a little.

Berkeley led the way into a game room, where a dozen or so boys were sitting around eating pizza with . . . Adrenaline Dennis.

I froze in my tracks. I was standing in the presence of *the* Adrenaline Dennis, and he was picking mushrooms off his pizza and putting them aside just like I did. Forget Apollo; I should've been named Adrenaline!

"This is my friend Tim from school," I heard Berkeley say. "He just got done with a Greek folk dance at the Museum of Science and Industry."

I gestured to my outfit. "But sometimes I like to wear this for just lounging around the house."

Several of the other guys laughed. I noticed Ryan lingering in the back. He might have been looking pretty sharp in his new gear and hairstyle, but the frown on his face soured it all.

All the kids were staring at my outfit, but I didn't care. Adrenaline Dennis was walking right toward me with his hand extended.

"Nice to meet you, Tim. I've studied a few different types of dance, but not Greek. Maybe you can show me some steps later."

Adrenaline Dennis wanted me to dance for him!

"Wait, wait," I said, shaking my head. "You dance? I thought you were into motocross."

He grinned. "A guy can have more than one interest, right? I'm sure you don't just dance."

I matched his grin. "True."

"Alistair . . . I mean *Adrenaline* . . . is really good at ballet," said Berkeley. "He trained in Paris."

Adrenaline nodded. "It keeps me limber when I'm on the bike. I also do a lot of yoga."

In a million years I never thought I'd be talking to a famous athlete about Greek folk dancing or ballet or yoga. The other kids were all stepping closer, wanting to be part of the conversation but not sure how.

"Uh . . . you want to talk flexible. Mitchell can bend his fingers all the way back to touch his arm." I pointed to him.

Mitchell stepped forward shyly and showed off his talent.

"Wow! Very impressive," said Adrenaline.

"I can do the splits!" said someone else.

"I can hold my breath for two minutes!"

Soon, everyone was shouting out their unique talents except, of course, for Ryan, who was standing apart from the crowd. I walked over to him.

"Why don't you share your talent of

blackmail?" I asked. "Or mention how your aunt is dating a Greek folk dancer?"

Ryan glared at me. "That's a lie."

I shrugged and smiled. "Your aunt had a guy pick her up in a blue Civic earlier, right? That was my uncle. And my uncle is a Greek folk dancer." I crossed my arms. "Just like me."

"Yeah, well, you're lame and so is everyone at this party," he grumbled. "And so is my aunt. She's probably dating your stupid uncle to get back at me."

Even though Ryan was a world-class jerk, I actually felt kind of bad for him. He was so dead set on not being liked that he made himself unlikable.

"Your aunt loves you more than you think," I said. "She bakes you cookies and worries that you'll catch cold, and she shelters you and she feeds you and she has lots of pictures of you." I held my arms open. "You don't do all that for someone you don't care about."

I thought that maybe, like the Grinch, I might soften his hard lump of a heart and make it grow a little, or at least get a smile. Instead, Ryan narrowed his eyes and said, "How do you know she has pictures of me?"

"Servants get curious." I smiled and clapped him on the shoulder. "You look great with a mustache, by the way."

Then I walked back to join the conversation with Adrenaline Dennis and the others.

It was a good day to be Tim Antonides.

Dear In the Dark,

As a wise man once said, "Be who you are and say what you feel, because those who mind don't matter, and those who matter don't mind." In other words, it's time to be honest, but not just with your friends. Be honest with yourself. If you're not ashamed of who you are, you don't give anyone else a reason to be either. Know who you are and own who you are.

And if all else fails, tell a ton of ghost stories so everyone begs you to keep the night-light on.

Confidentially yours,

Tim Antonides

Acknowledgments

Always for family, friends, and God.

For Annie, my editor, and Jenn, my agent, who, even after reading the silly things I write, haven't had me dragged away in a straitjacket.

For Frank Zahradnik, who is wise beyond my years and is always willing to talk.

For Katie and Shayda, my Wednesday night writing crew, who listened to me talk ad nauseam about the best way to blackmail someone.

For Kaiya and Killian, who always make me laugh and have a wonderful innocence about them.

For Shawn and Rena Bruman, who remind me to never give up hope.

And for the makers of See's Candies, who I'm pretty sure I single-handedly keep in business.

Turn the page for a sneak peek at the next book
in the Confidentially Yours series:

1

The Woman in the Cottage

It was a dark and stormy night . . .

Actually, it was a cold and snowy day, but no scary adventure ever starts like that. Unless there's a killer snowman. And even *that's* only scary until someone throws hot cocoa at him.

Anyway, why was I hoping for horror? Because so far my winter break had been dull with a capital ZZZZ. You'd think life in the Chicago suburbs would give me tons of stories to tell, but my most exciting news was Hammie and Chelsea, my cats, playing hide-and-seek in the Christmas tree.

Pine tree peekaboo: the highlight of my break.

Meanwhile my friends had awesome stories from their winter vacations. Heather Schwartz, one of my BFFs, had been in the spotlight on a holiday parade float with her choir, and Vanessa Jackson, my other bestie, had gone to Disney World with her brother and mom.

But I was probably most jealous of my friend Tim Antonides.

Not long ago, Tim became buddies with Berkeley Dennis, one of the richest and coolest kids at Abraham Lincoln Middle School. That alone wasn't very exciting, but Berkeley's cousin happened to be motocross superstar Adrenaline Dennis! He came to town for the holidays and took Berkeley and Tim to watch him practice for the X Games.

Heather and Vanessa couldn't have cared less when Tim bragged about going, but I was super jealous. I like sports just as much as he does. In fact, I give sports advice for Lincoln's Letters, the advice column at the *Lincoln Log*, my school newspaper. *Plus,* I'm captain of my soccer team, the Berryville Strikers. But I didn't even bother asking Tim if he could score me an invite. I got a major dudes-only vibe from the whole thing . . . mainly because Tim said, "It'll be dudes only."

So when another friend, Katie Kestler, asked if I wanted to visit a fortune-teller with her the day before spring semester, I instantly said, "Yes! Please! I'm about to start dressing up the cats!"

It was easy to talk Vanessa into coming since she's usually up for anything, but Heather was a little harder to convince. In fact, she still had doubts after Katie's mom, Bobbi, parked in front of a cottage with a wooden sign that read, "Madame Delphi: Seer Extraordinaire."

"Are we sure this is a good idea?" asked

Heather, eyeing some gargoyles on either side of the front door. "I mean . . . what if we accidentally summon something?"

"Don't worry. Madame Delphi's a professional who can handle anything," said Bobbi. "And I'll be right here waiting, so you can run out any time."

Heather didn't look reassured but opened the car door anyway.

"Tell Madame I said hi!" Bobbi called as my friends and I got out. "And that she was right about avoiding the salmon!"

I glanced back as Katie closed the car door and waved to her mom. "Why isn't she coming with us?" I asked.

"Bobbi has to make a conference call," said Katie, "and Madame Delphi only likes disembodied voices that come from spirits."

Heather spun toward us, nostrils flared. "So there *are* going to be ghosts?"

"Of course not," said V, putting a hand on her arm.

"But if there were, that would be awesome!" I charged through the snow and up the front steps, each plank of wood squeaking under my weight. "This place is creepy!"

"That's what bothers me." Heather shivered in her puffy green coat.

"Oh come on," Katie coaxed, putting an arm through one of Heather's. "It's a new year. Don't you want to know what's going to happen?"

I knocked on the front door, which opened by itself.

Heather turned to Katie. "Will I even live to see it?"

Vanessa stepped up to Heather's other side. "Don't worry, we'll be right here with you. The whole time."

Then V slipped and fell on her butt.

I cringed, Katie and Heather gasped, but

Vanessa lay back in the snow and laughed.

Even when she's down, she's smiling.

"How the heck did that happen?" I asked while Katie and Heather helped her up. "The snow isn't slippery."

"No, but the bottoms of my boots are." V lifted a foot just high enough for us to see that the sole was worn smooth.

"Hmm. Time to trash those," said Heather.

Vanessa and Katie gasped in unison.

"Are you insane?" asked Katie.

"They're vintage Dior!" added Vanessa.

The two of them are a little crazy for clothes. They're working on their own designer label, KV Fashions, and Vanessa offers style advice for Lincoln's Letters.

That's right; Vanessa writes the column, too, along with Heather and Tim! V, Heather, and I actually came up with the idea, since we'd been giving one another advice for years. Vanessa answers questions about beauty and fashion, I handle sports and fitness, Tim contributes the guy's point of view, and Heather fixes friendships and relationships because she has a way with people.

Like right now.

Instead of rolling her eyes, which was what I was doing, Heather said, "You know, if those boots are special, you might want to wait and wear them in the spring. Otherwise the water from the snow could wreck them."

Vanessa's eyes widened, and she lifted one foot off the ground, balancing precariously on the other like a fashionable flamingo.

"Oh for crying out loud," I said, leaping off the porch and running over to her. Unlike my glamorous friend, I was wearing appropriate winter clothes: real snow boots, jeans, and a thermal jacket. I turned my back to Vanessa and crouched to give her a piggyback ride. "Come on, V. The future awaits!"

She laughed and climbed on. "Don't drop me!" she warned.

I trudged up the steps with her, Heather hesitantly followed, and Katie ran ahead to push the door open the rest of the way.

Instead of the usual chimes to announce visitors, a harp strummed, giving our entrance a mystical feel. Goose bumps covered my arms, despite the fact that I was wearing a coat *and* a Vanessa. She slid off my back, boots thumping on the wooden floor, and said, "Whoa, check this place out!"

It took my eyes a minute to adjust to the darkened room. At one point it'd probably been several rooms, but the dividing walls had been knocked out and just a few support columns remained. The windows were covered with heavy velvet curtains, and the only light came from flickering oil lamps attached to the walls.

"This place is straight out of a movie," I murmured. "I love it."

"Can we please get this over with?" asked Heather, standing as close to the front door as she could without physically being a part of it.

"My mom says Madame usually has people wait in either the sitting area or gift shop," said Katie. "So I think she'll come get us when she's ready."

"Ooh." I rubbed my hands together excitedly. "How will she know we're here? Will a spirit from the beyond tell her?"

"More like a security camera from the ceiling," said V, pointing at an orb mounted above us.

"Aww." I lowered my hands.

Katie grinned at me. "Just pretend it's an all-seeing eye," she said in a spooky voice.

I snickered and glanced around. The sitting area to our left was decorated with a dumpy couch and chairs that had cracked seat cushions. The gift shop area was to the right and crowded with tables and bookshelves and spinning racks, all filled with various mystical items sporting orange price stickers.

Needless to say, my friends and I were drawn to the right.

"What is all this stuff?" asked V, pulling a book titled *Blessings and Curses* from a shelf. She flipped to a random page. "'Give your enemy bad breath.'"

"How?" asked Heather, reading over her shoulder.

"Easy. Garlic." I ran my finger over the spines of the other books. "I wonder if Tim's read any of these."

He was obsessed with books, particularly the classics. Although something told me *Crockpot Love Potions* probably wasn't on his list.

I moved on to a table covered with boxes of

candles, packets of herbs, and little knickknacks. "Hey, anybody wanna play poker?" I asked, plucking a deck of cards from the pile.

Katie laughed. "Good luck with that. Those are tarot cards."

"Tarot cards?" I slid a couple out of the box. One of them had a guy in a jester's costume and was labeled "The Fool." The other, "The Tower," was just that: an image of a tower. "What is it, a matching game?"

She shook her head. "They're for telling fortunes."

I put the cards back and picked up a pocket-size horseshoe. "I'd like to see the horse who can wear this."

Somewhere behind us hinges creaked, and we all turned toward the sound. A tall, blond woman in a flowing purple dress shuffled in our direction from an open door between the oil lamps.

"Good afternoon. I am Madame Delphi," she said with a slight bow and a breathy voice. "I understand you wish to see the future."

"I actually wish to see a mirror," said V, wrapping a silky scarf around her neck. "Also, do you have this in blue?"

Heather elbowed her in the side, and Madame Delphi raised an eyebrow.

"Everything in the shop is as-is," she said. "Including my predictions." She pressed her fingertips together. "I must warn you that people can be disappointed by what I see. They beg for a different future." She shook her head, eyes locked on mine. "But your future will be what it will be."

Again, goose bumps.

"Now," she said in a soft voice, "who will go first?"

Katie hurried to the front as if Madame Delphi was handing out designer dresses. "Hi! I'm Katie

Kestler and you did a reading for my mom, Bobbi Kestler, and you told her to skip the salmon at a wedding and she did and everyone who ate it got food poisoning, but not her because she didn't eat it." Katie paused for oxygen. "So she said to tell you that you were right, and I am more than ready to have my fortune read!" She turned to the rest of us. "I mean . . . if that's okay."

V and I nodded.

"You can go for me, too," said Heather.

Madame Delphi arched a brow. "You fear the future?"

"No." Heather shrank back. "I fear this moment right now."

"Aww." I put an arm around her. "Heather, you don't have to go in if you don't want."

"Yeah." V bumped her. "We just thought this would be fun to do together."

"Well . . . I want to have fun," Heather said, nodding toward the door Madame Delphi had come through. "Is it even darker in there?"

Madame Delphi approached Heather and took her hands. "Let me make this easy. It won't be as accurate but . . ." She flipped Heather's hands to face palms up. "Are you left- or right-handed?"

"Left," said Heather, glancing curiously from her hands to Madame Delphi.

Madame Delphi studied Heather's palms for a moment and smiled. "My, you are a talent, aren't you?"

"She's an *amazing* singer," I chimed in.

Heather smiled and blushed. "I'm okay."

"Your talent will take you far," said Madame Delphi, tracing a finger along Heather's palm. "And you will live a long, happy life." She rested a hand on each of Heather's and stepped away. "There now. Was that so terrible?"

"Not at all," said Heather, beaming.

Katie scooted closer. "Is it my turn?"

Madame Delphi nodded. "Would you like—"

"The works!" exclaimed Katie, already bounding toward the open door.

Five minutes later Katie bounded back out to the sitting area where Heather, V, and I were waiting.

"Next!" she chirped.

"I'm guessing you got a good fortune?" I asked, looking up from the pack of tarot cards I was building into a house.

"Oh, not just me," said Katie. She flopped onto a couch next to Vanessa and raised a cloud of dust in the process. "Vanny too!"

Vanessa lowered the copy of *Natural Beauty* she was reading. "Your fortune included me?"

"Well . . . KV Fashions," Katie explained. She rubbed the thumb and fingertips of one hand together. "Madame Delphi said money's gonna flow like a river!" She nudged V. "Ask Madame Delphi about money, but don't tell her we work together. I guarantee she'll say we make more this year."

"Of course we will," said V with a smirk. "We can't possibly make less than last year's nothing."

We all laughed.

So far KV Fashions' only big business project had been makeovers for the Fall Into Winter dance, and the price had been a clothing item for charity. It was a sweet gesture, but afterward, V told me they'd given up about twenty-five bucks each in the process.

"Go on." Katie prodded V. "And try to get details, like what specifically makes us richety-rich." Her eyes sparkled.

V glanced down at where I was sitting on the floor. "Would it be okay if I went next? The future of KV Fashions may or may not be riding on this." She leaned closer. "I'm betting on 'not.'"

"I can hear you!" said Katie from over her shoulder.

"Sure," I said with a nod. "I've got the second story of my card house to work on anyway."

While V walked off to meet Madame Delphi, Heather moved from one of the cracked chairs to sit next to Katie on the couch.

"What else did she tell you?" asked Heather.

"Yeah, did you ask when you were going to die?" I chimed in.

Heather turned to me with wide eyes. "Brooke!"

"What? I'm going to ask when it's *my* turn. This woman can see the future! Why stop at 'Will I win the Women's World Cup?'"

Katie laughed. "It's fine. And no, I didn't ask because I already know I'm going to live to be super old. Everyone in my family does . . . except my great-grandpa Pete, who fell in a volcano."

Heather and I both raised our eyebrows.

"Okay, there's way more to *that* story," I said, putting down my cards.

When V emerged from the back room, it was to find me, Heather, and Katie laughing so hard we were crying. Even though she had no idea why, Vanessa joined in.

"Poor Pete," said Heather between giggles. "That banana sandwich just wasn't worth it."

We all calmed down, and I poked Vanessa in the side. "How was your time with the teller?"

"Fun!" she said. "We talked about fashion and Disney World."

Katie, Heather, and I looked at one another.

"What about your reading?" asked Katie.

"Well, I'm going to get less clumsy," she said, making a thumbs-up. "But she didn't mention anything about getting rich." She held up a finger. "Although there are about to be major changes in my love life."

"Ooh!" Heather rubbed her hands together. "Between you and Gil?"

Gil Pendleton was Vanessa's boyfriend, who

also happened to work at the *Lincoln Log* with us doing horoscopes and photography.

I narrowed my eyes in mock dismay. "V, I don't want to be on your reality show, *Middle School Marriage*."

Everyone started laughing again, including Vanessa, who placed her hands on her blushing cheeks.

"I could melt snow with my face right now!" she exclaimed.

Madame Delphi appeared in the doorway, and we quieted.

"We're so sorry!" said Katie. "We didn't mean to disturb the spirit world."

"It's all right. There was one more of you waiting to see me?" asked Madame Delphi.

"That's me!" I got to my feet and stepped over my tarot-card house.

Madame Delphi nodded and gestured for me to follow. I waved at my friends before stepping through the doorway into a smaller, even darker room.

"Please sit," said Madame Delphi, pointing to a small table with two chairs across from each other. There wasn't a crystal ball like I'd been expecting. Just another pack of tarot cards and a tea set.

I scooted my chair as close to the table as possible and placed both hands in the center, palms up. Now for the real excitement!

"I won't be reading your palms today," said Madame Delphi. "It is a very inexact practice."

"Oh." I withdrew my hands.

Madame Delphi reached for the teapot and poured hot water into a cup, placing it in front of me. I peered inside and saw leaves skittering along the bottom.

"Let that sit for a few minutes while we turn the cards," she said.

She passed them to me and asked me to

shuffle. "I need the cards to pick up your energy and presence."

I looked down at the cards. "Um . . . okay."

When I was done, she had me spread the cards facedown across the table.

"Choose three," she said. "To represent your past, present, and future."

I selected three and handed them to her. As she turned them over, she explained what they meant.

"The Strength card reveals you have accomplished much."

I sat a little straighter in my chair and puffed out my chest. "Yep!"

"The Three of Pentacles means you are currently in a position where you must collaborate and work well with others."

"I'm the team leader for my advice column and captain of my soccer team," I said.

She nodded. "Your cards represent you well."

Madame Delphi flipped the last card and gasped.

"What?" I asked.

"Your future," she said, "is represented by the Nine of Swords!" In a softer voice she added, "The lord of cruelty."

That didn't sound promising.

"What . . . what does that mean?" I managed to squeak out.

"Great sorrow and grief," said Madame Delphi. . . .